11/5/00

For
Roszena

"May you be consoled in the
secret symmetry of your soul!"
Rasy Mama

Why Monkeys Live in Trees
and Other Stories from Benin

by Raouf Mama

with drawings by
Andy Jones

Curbstone Press

printed in Canada on acid-free paper by Transcontinental
Cover design: Stone Graphics
Cover image: A. Jones

This book was published with the support of the
Connecticut Commission on Culture and Tourism, the
National Endowment for the Arts, and donations from
many individuals. We are very grateful for this
support.

Library of Congress Cataloging-in-Publication Data

    Mama, Raouf, 1956-
    Why monkeys live in trees and other stories from Benin / by Raouf
Mama ; with drawings by Andy Jones. — 1st ed.
        p. cm.
    ISBN-13: 978-1-931896-21-4 (pbk. : alk. paper)
    ISBN-10: 1-931896-21-6 (pbk. : alk. paper)
    1. Tales—Benin. 2. Folklore—Benin. I. Title.
    GR351.4.M36 2006
    398.2'096683—dc22

                                        2006017585

published by
    CURBSTONE PRESS   321 Jackson St.   Willimantic, CT 06226
        phone: 860-423-5110   e-mail: info@curbstone.org
                        www.curbstone.org

Acknowledgements

Why Monkeys Live in Trees was many, many years in the making and took the kindness and benevolent support of many to come to fruition. I am unable to name all those who have played a part in the making of this book, but I want to single out a few for a special tribute of gratitude.

My thanks go forth to my family for their patience and understanding, to Professor Lyall Powers, my mentor, and to his wife Loretta Powers, for listening to the stories and providing feedback, to my students at Eastern Connecticut State University and elsewhere for helpful response to the stories. I am grateful to the Connecticut State University System for financial assistance, to my colleagues and friends for their interest and encouragement, and to Jane Blanshard, Janet Dauphin, Judy Doyle, Bob Smith, Sandy Taylor, and Jantje Tielken for their superb editorial and publicity work. I want to thank all my teachers for everything they have taught me and Dr. Niara Sudarkasa for throwing open to me the gates of graduate school, where I first decided to become a writer and a collector of tales.

Finally, I owe a debt of gratitude to the storytellers whose stories I have retold in this book: Mr. Sylvain Agossou, Mr. Balogoun, Mr. Cyril Biaou, Mrs. Rabiatou Ghezodje, my elder mother (may her soul rest in Peace), Mrs. Victoire Guezodje, Mrs. Martine Hounsou, Mr. Ali Sabi, and Mr. Arthur Sevi. Just as you instructed, entertained, and inspired me through your stories, may all who read or hear *Why Monkeys Live In Trees* derive from it some instruction, some entertainment, and some inspiration.

CONTENTS

Trickster and Sacred Tales From Benin
AN INTRODUCTION

The West African Republic of Benin, formerly called Dahomey, is gifted with a great folktale tradition, one of the most beautiful in Africa. In the years of my childhood, my favorite pastime was to sit with the family in the evening after the evening meal and listen, as my mother, my stepmother, or an elder told with splendid eloquence stories of long ago. There was no television then, and stories were our souls' daily bread. We were treated to sacred tales, trickster tales, ghost stories, legends, and "pourquoi" tales, that is, tales furnishing explanations of various customs and natural phenomena.

Those tales brought to life a colorful array of characters: kings, queens, princes and princesses, peasants, merchants, hunters, orphans, twins, birds of the air, beasts of the field, and creatures of the deep. In those stories human beings, animals, plants, as well as spirits interacted on a daily basis. All the stories had morals. Vice was always punished and virtue rewarded.

By the time I turned sixteen, however, the time-honored tradition of evening story time in the family had all but faded out of existence. The neocolonial educational system, which sought to cut us off from our roots, the advent of TV, the spread of technology, urbanization, and economic hardship have all played a part in the demise of that tradition. And with its passing a great source of entertainment and spiritual nourishment and a powerful educational medium has been lost.

The twelve tales in this collection include trickster tales such as "Why Monkeys Live in Trees" as well as sacred tales such as "The Magic of Love." Unlike my first book of Beninese stories, *Why Goats Smell Bad and Other Stories from Benin,* not a single trickster tale in *Why Monkeys Live in Trees* features Yogbo the Glutton, the archetypal trickster figure of the Fon oral tradition. The reason for this is twofold: first, although Yogbo the Glutton is the most common trickster figure in the Fon folktale tradition, there are a few others, including Tortoise, Hare, and Monkey. Second, whereas all the stories in *Why Goats Smell Bad* are exclusively from the Fon people, the stories in *Why Monkeys Live in Trees* come from a wide range of Beninese ethnic groups, including the Adja from the west, the Batonou from the north, and the Chabe from the central region of Benin. The tricksters in those stories do not have Yogbo the Glutton's supernatural stature, nor do they share the mark of gluttony that makes Yogbo such a humorous figure. They match Yogbo the Glutton in cunning, however, and their stories are no less humorous.

Another interesting difference between the two books is that no sacred tale in *Why Monkeys Live in Trees* bears as distinct a mark of the Judeo–Christian tradition as does "The King Who Would Be God" in *Why Goats Smell Bad*. "The Jar and The Necklace," however, is reminiscent of the Old Testament principle of "an eye for an eye," and "The Prodigal Prince" bears a certain resemblance to the tale of the Prodigal Son.

I collected and retold these stories over a period of eight years. In translating and retelling them in English, I gave them titles, for Beninese folktales have no titles, and I provided description in an attempt to bring them alive. These are the main contributions I have made to the stories in this book. As pieces of oral literature and cultural history, these tales shed light on some of the values and beliefs as well as the customs and traditions of the people of Benin. And they sound a similar note to that of folktales from all over the world: for all our differences, the human race is one color, which is the color of blood. Like the other folktales from the unnumbered multitude of the communities making up the human family, these tales bear testimony to the truth of a poem titled "Underneath, We're All the Same," written by a sixteen-year-old girl from Indiana named Amy Maddox:

He prayed—it was not my religion.
He ate—it was not what I ate.

He spoke—it was not my language.
He dressed—it was not what I wore.
He took my hand—it was not the color of mine
But when he laughed, it was how I laughed.
And when he cried, it was how I cried.

If we will listen with our hearts—our inner ears—to the voice of the narrators in these stories, we will realize that, in spite of everything, we have the same joys and sorrows, the same hopes and the same fears, that we are, all of us, vulnerable to death, and disease, and the passing of time. We will realize that the human race indeed is one color, the color of blood.

—Raouf Mama

Dedication

To my children—Faridath, Rabiath, Gemilath, Raman, and Rahim—for the gift of Joy.

To my nephew Ousmane Mama for the gift of Love.

To Josias, Loth, and Mestchak Mevognon for the gift of Friendship.

To the late Professor Jossou Marie-Cecile for the gift of Learning.

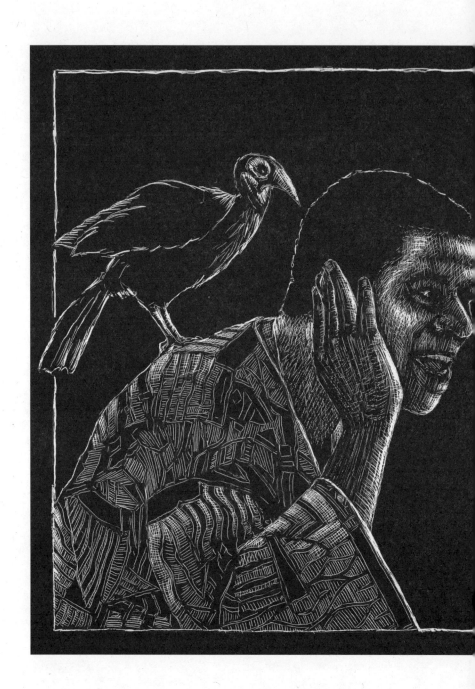

Come and Hear My Story

Come and hear my story, come so that you and I
May fly on the wings of memory back to the years of my childhood,
When I used to sit with the family in the evening and listen
As my mother, my stepmother, or my grandfather told stories of long ago.
Come and sit and listen, as I used to sit and listen in those days,
When there was no TV, and stories were our souls' daily bread.
Come and sit and listen, for stories are magical
They are a journey and a joining.
In a story, we go to new places, we meet new people, and we learn new ideas,
And they become our places, our people, our ideas.
Stories give you and me a means of talking to each other about each other.
Come and sit and listen, for I sing of the dignity of man,
The wonder of life, and the oneness of the human race.
Come and sit and listen, with your inner ears, for only then will you hear
The roar on the other side of silence.
Come and listen, for stories teach simple truths that may widen the wisdom of kings.
Come and sit and listen, for listening is the key to learning and understanding.

Blessed Are the Storytellers,
For They Are the Keepers of the Word

Blessed are the storytellers, for to them God gave the gift of eloquence,
That their words may go forth to the four corners of the earth,
Charged with the fire of passion and the wisdom of the ages,
Making the deaf to hear and the blind to see.
Blessed are the storytellers, for in the magic circle of the storyteller's art
We enter into the drama of the human heart
With its joys and sorrows,
Its laughter and its tears,
Its hopes and its fears.
There we see and we feel the noonday brightness
Of the human capacity for love,
And we plumb the darkest depths of our potential for evil.
There we are moved to roll back the frontier of darkness,
And strike a blow against prejudice and man's inhumanity to man.
Blessed are the storytellers, for through them
We can tame the savagery of man and make gentle the life of this world.
Blessed are the storytellers, for they are the keepers of the word.

Why Monkeys Live in Trees

Once upon a time the jungle was gripped by a terrible drought. For months and months not a drop of rain fell from heaven, and in the sky the sun blazed fiercely day in, day out. The birds of the air and the beasts of the field performed ceremony after ceremony to bring back the rain, but it was all in vain. One after another the lakes and the rivers turned to mud, and everywhere the lush grass gradually faded from bright green to dull brown. Soon, the tall leafy trees lost their leaves and stood like grief-stricken giants raising a thousand gnarled and withered hands toward the heavens.

With growing alarm, the inhabitants of the jungle saw their provisions dwindle to nothing. It was only a matter of time before they all starved to death!

Soon, hunger spoiled the animals' temper. It wasn't long before everyone's hand was raised against his neighbor.

And strife, joining hands with hunger, made life in the jungle an ordeal and a hazard.

Lion, king of the jungle, looked out of his den one day and noted with great sadness what a wasteland the jungle had become. Not a birdsong was to be heard, and the few animals to be seen here and there all wore expressions of haunting, unendurable despair.

"Things cannot go on like this much longer," Lion sighed. "I must call an emergency meeting of all the inhabitants of the jungle to see what we can do together to save ourselves from death."

The next day all the animals gathered for a debate on the drought.

Surveying the assembled multitude with sad, imploring eyes, Lion said, "Unless the jungle soon puts an end to the drought, the drought will surely put an end to the jungle! But how is one to prevent the unthinkable?"

"The drought has defied our rain makers' magic, and made life in our realm a nightmare!" Elephant said, raising a thin, withered trunk in the air as evidence of the general plight.

"And God the Creator has turned a deaf ear to our prayers and supplications," Monkey added, his chin cupped in the palm of his hand, his forehead creased with worry.

"Let's send someone to Heaven to plead for God's help," Eagle observed, pointing his beak upward as if to show the way.

"That is the only thing we haven't tried so far," Squirrel said, nodding several times to give emphasis to his words.

"You have spoken truly," Lion said. "The only thing we haven't done yet is send one of us to speak to the Creator!"

There followed a lively debate in the course of which various animals were proposed for the heavenly mission. In the end, Monkey was chosen for he was considered the smartest and the most eloquent of all.

So Monkey went up to heaven and, standing before the throne of God, he said:

I have come on a mission of last resort, oh Lord of life!
To seek relief for my fellow creatures' desperate plight!
Bid the hunger and the drought cease, we humbly pray!
Let there be food, water, and an end to neighborly strife,
that we may not hunt and kill each other for our prey!

As Monkey spoke, God fixed him with a look of infinite sadness and sat nodding to himself long after he had fallen silent. Then, He said:

4

This very moment do I bid the drought cease,
And from your terrible plight grant you release.
Food and drink you shall take back to your kind.
Share it wisely so that everyone relief may find.

When Monkey took leave of the Heavenly Host and came back to earth, he saw a jungle arrayed in colors of dazzling light—red, yellow, green, blue, and spotless white. The rain had come back and quickened to new life his jungle home and all that was in it. Once again the grass was bright green, flowers were in bloom, and the lakes and the rivers were filled to the brim with sparkling, sun-flecked water.

Following Monkey's return, Lion called another meeting. Then Monkey led the assembled multitude to the spot where the angels had stored the food that God had sent to soothe their hunger: It was a breathtaking sight: Countless barns filled with food of all kinds: big fresh-picked mangoes, papayas, guavas, bananas, oranges, luscious vegetables, succulent nuts and grains. The animals could hardly contain their joy. Here was enough food to feed them all the days of their lives, while they were expecting just enough to save them from hunger. God was indeed a merciful, infinitely compassionate God.

And while all the animals were skipping for joy, Monkey told them that God had entrusted him with the distribution of the food and that he intended to fulfil his God-given duty immediately.

With a mischievous gleam in his eyes, Monkey settled down to the task of distribution.

To some he gave so much it was obscene, and to others he gave so little it was pitiful. To some he gave just enough, and to others he gave nothing at all. Soon, there was a terrible uproar. Almost everybody was complaining, even those who had nothing to complain about. But the strangest thing of all was that the loudest complaints came from some of those to whom Monkey had been the most generous. To his utter amazement, they argued that they, too, needed more!

It wasn't long before the gates of Heaven were crowded with beasts and birds clamoring for God to punish Monkey for gross injustice. In the end, God had to come down to earth to hear the case against Monkey and do something to restore calm to the jungle.

For hours God listened patiently as Monkey's neighbors complained against him.

Then, God turned to Monkey and said, "What have you to say for yourself?"

With your own ears, you have heard,
The same as I, each and every word:
To some you gave so much it was obscene,
To some, so little it was downright mean.
To some, a fair share of what the angels brought,
And to some you gave absolutely naught!

And to that, Monkey replied:

Lend me an ear, Dispenser of all things, I pray.
Before You judge, ponder what I have to say.
To some You give health, wealth, and children without number.
To some You give glory, fame, and fortune, power and valor,
So that they live a life of considerable comfort and ease,
But to some You give nothing or precious little of these.

This, then, is my plea:

To some I gave so much it was obscene,
to some, so little it was downright mean.
To some I gave a fair share of what the angels brought,

and to some I gave absolutely naught.
But I have only practiced what You Yourself have taught!

A faint smile flickered across God's face, but He was in no mood to let Monkey go free. So He said:

Your plea is but a thin cover for mischief-making and pride.
For failing to make justice, love, and humility your guide,
a wanderer shall you be forever in your jungle home.
You and your seed I condemn to wander and roam,
For playing God and seeking yourself to please.
From this day forward, your dwelling shall be in the trees.
And to the children you shall be a thing of sport.
From their mischief you shall have no resort.

And so it has been, to this day.

Why the Sun Shines by Day
and the Moon by Night

My story takes flight, over countries and kingdoms of long ago back to the beginning of the Universe, when the Sun and the Moon were friends. Both were creatures of light and both had made their dwellings in the heavens from where they gave light to the world and all that lived in it. The sun and the moon had more children than any other creature on earth or in heaven, thousands and thousands of them. And whenever they visited each other or went for a stroll across the sky, surrounded by their beautiful children, it was a sight to behold! Tens of thousands of bright little creatures skipping, jumping, romping about and having fun under the watchful gaze of two splendid figures arrayed in light and walking side by side, chatting merrily and scattering moon glimmer and sunbeams all around.

Catching the magic of the hour, the green grass, the leafy trees, and the many-colored flowers would sparkle with light; the rivers, the lakes, and the boundless sea would turn to a thousand shimmering mirrors, and the air would ring with exquisite melodies from songbirds and the laughter of men, women, and children at play.

Now, the special friendship between the sun and the moon was a great wonder to the world, for never had two creatures so different in character been united by so strong a bond of friendship. The sun was hot, fiery-tempered, and bold, whereas the moon was cool, mild-mannered, and secretive. What was more, the sun was constant in purpose and suspicious of change, whereas the moon was impulsive and fond of change. In fact the moon was known on earth and in heaven as the lady of a thousand faces, moods, and shapes.

One day, the moon told the sun:

My children are a constant headache to me!
I am at my wits' end, I know not what to do!
I am sure yours are really troublesome, too
Let all the little brats be thrown into the sea!
None is better placed to do the deed than we!

The sun remained deep in thought a moment, and then said:

My children have given me more trouble than I can say.
Many times, I had secretly resolved to cast them away
But simply couldn't bring myself to do the terrible deed.
Readily will I fling them into the sea if you take the lead!

The next day at dawn, the moon, followed by the sun, quickly made her way to the shore of the sea. The two friends were veiled in mist, and each was holding a huge bag almost bursting at the seams. First the moon, then the sun threw their loads into the ocean and retraced their steps. The heavy bags bobbed up and down a moment and were lost to sight.

For many days the sun and the moon shut themselves up in their homes, as though unable to face the world after what they had done to their own children. No one in heaven or earth had any idea what had become of the moon, the sun, and their beautiful children. And while they remained out of sight, heaven and earth were shrouded in thick darkness, a mournful silence weighed everything down, and there was in the air fear of an impending catastrophe. Then, on the seventh day, the sun boldly came out, vowing to come clean and get on with her life.

That was when she had the shock of her life! For in the vast playing field of Heaven, she caught sight of the moon surrounded by her children, thousands upon thousands of radiant creatures, glittering and shimmering like so many priceless jewels! The sun shook her head and rubbed her eyes again and again, believing herself to be the plaything of a cruel fantasy. She stood staring a long time, her eyes bulging out, her hair standing on end.

Then, it slowly dawned on her that the moon had lied to her and that the bag she had thrown into the sea contained not her children at all but stones and pebbles! Her eyes flashed red, and her mouth opened wide in a long-drawn, blood-curdling cry that sent the moon and her children flying in all directions, like dry leaves blown by the wind.

"You monster of a witch," she screamed, "cursed be the day on which I called you friend and placed my trust in you. You made me send my children to a watery grave at the bottom of the sea, but you have protected and retained your own!" Foaming at the mouth, the sun went after the moon, and soon, the two former friends, now mortal enemies, were locked in a terrible battle, biting, scratching, punching, and kicking each other. That was the first eclipse.

While they fought, heaven and earth were enveloped in darkness, and there was nothing their inhabitants could do to stop the fight. In the end, the elders, having consulted the oracle, ordered the people to get calabashes, gourds, bowls, and dishes—any utensils they could lay their hands on—and beat them with sticks and stones, with all their strength. The people did, and a great noise and clamor rose to the heavens and finally drew the sun and the moon apart. From that day onward, they have avoided each other's company, and the sun has shone by day and the moon by night; the children of the moon, the *Sounvi* or stars, too, have shone by night and lived in mortal terror of the sun.

The sun has lived a solitary life ever since, pacing, pacing the boundless dome of heaven from east to west and back again, grieving for her children that are no more. So heartbreaking was the plight of the sun that the Creator took pity on her and turned her children into multitudes of fish or *Huevi* to be found in the sea and in rivers and lakes throughout the world. Among these there was a fish, unlike any other, called *Zokin*. She was the only child of her own that the moon had put in the bag she had filled with stones and pebbles and cast into the sea.

All this happened long, long ago, at the beginning of time, but the sun still bears the moon a mortal grudge to this day. The sight of the moon's beautiful children, glittering and shimmering like priceless jewels, is a daily torment to the sun; and sometimes, when she can bear it no longer, she goes after the moon and engages her in combat. While the two of them are locked in battle, there is darkness on the face of the earth. That's when people take to beating dishes, bowls, calabashes, and gourds with sticks and stones in keeping with an ancient belief in the power of the noise and clamor thus produced to end an eclipse and stop the fight between the sun and the moon. And so it has been, to this day.

Why Bee Makes Honey and
Snake Crawls on Its Belly

My story takes flight, over countries and kingdoms of long ago, back to the beginning of time, and alights on two brothers: Snake and Bee. They were tillers of the soil and lived with their widowed mother in a village on the shore of a mighty river.

Every year their farm yielded abundant crops of corn, potatoes, yams, cassava, and vegetables, for the soil was rich and rain was plentiful.

It came to pass, however, that the rain failed, the river sank to its lowest level, and the yield of their farm dwindled to nothing.

Bee, Snake, and their mother soon fell on hard times and knew not where to turn.

One day, Dove, their friend, heard of their misfortune and came flying from her village on the other side of the river to offer help, saying:

> *Pack up your belongings and come with me,*
> *To a country far away on the shore of the sea!*
> *There you shall find wealth, joy, and peace of mind!*
> *It is a land of opportunity, the only one of its kind!*

Dove's words brought hope and comfort to Bee and Snake, but, sadly, their mother was too old to go. So it was decided that Bee and Snake should leave their mother behind, but must provide for her all the days of her life.

On taking leave of their mother, Snake and Bee were very sad and a little afraid of what the future held for them. As they took flight, with Dove leading the way, they sang an old song to keep up their courage:

Before we leave our home for a foreign shore,
We always prepare long and hard, as if for war.
Before we leave our home for a foreign land
We work hard, and leave nothing unplanned.

The country where the travelers finally landed was just as bountiful and welcoming as Dove had described it. Bee soon found favor with the king and quickly became one of his most trusted advisors. As the saying went in the land, "Bee has the king's ear, and he who wants to talk to the king must first talk to Bee."

As far as Snake was concerned, he set up business as a baker and his cornbread was famed throughout the land for its sweetness. But whereas Bee always sent their mother food, beautiful clothes, and jewelry, Snake completely forgot about her.

One day, a messenger came to Bee and Snake and told them that their mother was ill and wanted to see them urgently. Bee wasted no time in setting out, but it took Snake many days to make up his mind. He didn't like the idea of entrusting his prosperous cornbread business to someone else. "If mother's illness hasn't killed her so far, surely it can wait a few more days," Snake reasoned as he worried about what was going to happen to his business when he was gone.

When Snake finally decided to go, his mother was near death. Bee had done all he could to comfort her and make her last days on earth as happy as they could be, but she couldn't help weeping over Snake's abandonment of her.

"You have come at last, but you might just as well have stayed away, for my days on earth are over," the mother wailed as Snake approached her sickbed.

She had changed beyond recognition. In place of the lively and beautiful mother he once knew, Snake saw a being ravaged by disease, with a careworn face and arms and legs as thin as sticks. It was then that Snake realized how cruel he had been to his mother. He wanted to say something to soothe his mother's anger and make up for all the years of neglect, but his tongue failed him.

And as he stood there, his head bowed in shame, the mother went on:

I love you more than the very breath of life,
But my love you have repaid with cruelty.
For this, you and all Creation shall be at strife.
You and your kind shall crawl on your belly.

No sooner had the mother spoken those fateful words than Snake's body underwent an extraordinary transformation. His arms and legs withered and vanished from sight, and he changed into a rope-like creature all covered with shiny scales. His forked tongue darted in and out of his oddly shaped head while his tiny eyes burned like fire. And while Bee looked on in horror, Snake went slithering out of the house, hissing and twisting, and was soon lost to sight.

Then the mother turned to Bee and said:

You have given me peace and happiness in my old age
For all that you have done for me, this shall be your wage:
You and your kind, the world shall forever hold in high esteem
And they shall find the fruit of your labor pleasing in the
extreme.

And so it was that Bee and its kind came to be producers of honey. To this day, when a man or a woman finds something exceedingly sweet, they say simply, "it is sweet as honey."

How Goat Got out of Trouble

My story takes flight over countries and kingdoms of long ago and alights on Goat. Now, Goat was a well-known healer and a skillful builder, and he had just built a house. It was made of smooth mud walls and covered with a thatched roof that shone and glittered in the sun. It was big and it was beautiful, just as Goat had wanted it, for he was about to get married and had always dreamed of a beautiful house for himself, his beloved, and their children.

In those days, it was the custom to consult the oracle before building a house. So Goat paid tortoise, the diviner, a visit, and this is what tortoise said:

Your house will rouse some to joy and some to anger.
It shall bring you praise and it shall put you in danger.
To ward off danger, keep in your house plenty of honey.
Mark my words! One day, it just might come in handy.

As soon as the house was completed, Goat got a gourd filled with honey, kept it ready to hand, and waited. As tortoise had foretold, Goat's new house brought him much praise. It was the talk of the forest, and birds and beasts came from near and far to look at it and compliment Goat. Goat enjoyed the praise, but tortoise's warning against danger made him cautious and fearful. "Where is the danger to come from, and how is honey going to overcome it?" he would wonder, his heart beating fast.

One day, Goat was napping after weeding and cleaning his yard all morning under a blazing sun when he was startled awake by a cold, raspy voice calling out a greeting. Jumping to his feet, Goat rushed to the door and poked his head out.

"Good afternoon, Hyena!" Goat cried out. Goat knew that

Hyena was a mean, unfriendly fellow and that his visit was a portent of trouble. Tortoise's words sounded in Goat's ears as he thought of something to say:

Your house shall rouse some to joy and some to anger.
It shall bring you praise and it shall put you in danger.

"Come in and make yourself at home while I bring you water," Goat said, feigning great joy at seeing Hyena. Hyena, however, took no notice of Goat's show of friendliness.

"I will certainly make myself at home; as for water, let's not waste time; I will get it when I need it!" he growled, impatiently waving Goat to a seat.

"Your house is very beautiful," he went on, his eyes blazing like fire. "It's too beautiful, in fact, for a creature like you. Lion, king of the jungle, doesn't have a house like this. Not even I, the smartest of all, live in a house like this. I want your house, and I shall have it. If you want to fight for it, I am ready, but if I were you, I would think twice before getting up to any foolishness."

Goat broke out in a cold sweat. He cast a lingering, despairing look around his beautiful house, thinking of all the hard work it had cost him. He thought of the wife and the children he had wanted to share it with and felt as though his dreams were collapsing all around him.

"Have mercy," he cried in a tearful, imploring voice. "Let me keep this house and I shall build you one more beautiful still."

"Build that one for yourself," Hyena replied, smiling ferociously. "This one is good enough for me."

"But you cannot have this house!" Goat cried, stamping his feet, his anger getting the better of his terror for a few, fleeting moments.

18

"I will have it whether you like it or not!" Hyena growled, baring his sharp teeth.

"No, you will not!"

"Yes, I will!"

"No, you will not!"

"Enough!" Hyena screamed, rushing upon Goat. He was about to sink his claws into his neck when he was startled by a roaring greeting broken by dry, terrible coughs, "Good…after…noon!"

Hyena backed away and thrust his head out the door to see who it was.

"I say…good…after…noon…" Lion roared again, coughing and spluttering.

"Are you all right?" Hyena inquired, struggling to hide his annoyance at Lion's untimely interruption.

"You see me…in this…state…and you ask if I am…all right!" Lion growled, gasping for breath.

"I am sorry you are sick," said Goat, who had come out to join Hyena. To Goat, Lion's arrival was a godsend, and his joy and relief stood between him and Hyena like a yawning gap.

"Your sorrow…won't do me…any good…unless you have medicine…that can cure this dreadful cough…I have had for a whole week now. I am so sick…I am almost at…the point of death. Do you have a cure?"

Both Hyena and Goat remained silent while Lion looked expectantly from one to the other, breathing heavily.

All of a sudden, Goat's face lit up and he said with a faint, cunning smile playing about his lips:

"As a matter of fact, I have a cure."

"Let me have it!" Lion cried, jumping up and grabbing Goat by the shoulders as though to stop him from melting into thin air.

"I have a cure if you will provide the main ingredient," Goat said cunningly, "but I don't think you can get it."

"Tell me what you need and I shall pursue it to the ends of the earth, if I have to!" Lion roared, his eyes burning with fierce determination.

"Just a moment," Goat said and went back into his house. Shortly thereafter he reemerged, holding aloft a gourd filled with honey. "If you provide the lungs and heart of a healthy hyena," Goat said, "I will prepare the most potent cough medicine on the face of the earth!"

"The heart and lungs of a hyena," Hyena cried, gripping his chest as though to prevent anyone from snatching his heart and lungs away. "The heart and lungs of a hyena! I have never heard such nonsense in my life!"

"You won't let me die, will you?" Lion said, fixing Hyena with a chilling, icy gaze.

"Let you die! Let you die! What about me?" Hyena cried, gesturing wildly.

"Come on," Lion snarled, "it's just your heart and lungs I'm asking for! Come on!"

"My heart and lungs! We shall see about that!" Hyena screamed, taking to his heels, his teeth clenched tight, his tail tucked between his legs.

Quick as a flash, Lion went after Hyena in hot pursuit.

"Lion! Lion!" Goat shouted triumphantly, jumping up and down. "Give me Hyena's heart and lungs and I shall give you the most potent cough medicine on earth!"

Long after Lion and Hyena had vanished from sight, Goat went on jumping up and down and shouting at the top of his lungs, until he grew hoarse and was drenched in sweat.

Then, he went back into his house, muttering to himself

with a self-satisfied smile, "Lion will keep Hyena's mind off my house for a while."

Well, Hyena gave Goat no further trouble. To thank Tortoise for the part he had played in saving him from danger, Goat befriended him and made him a guest of honor at his wedding.

And whereas Hyena lived in fear and on the run, Goat and his wife lived happily into old age, surrounded by their children, grandchildren, and great-grandchildren.

Truth and Lie

Long ago, when the world was new, Truth and Lie lived in the same village. Lie was tall, a little fat, and had a big belly. He was of delicate health, for he suffered from heart disease and shortness of breath. Now Lie was a smooth talker. Always dressed in beautiful but cheap clothes, he could talk a miser into exchanging a pot of gold for a handful of dirt. Lie was very popular and made friends easily, although rumor had it that he was not to be trusted, that he would abandon a friend at the least sign of trouble.

Truth was lean and well-proportioned and had clear, bright eyes. He was a man of few words. Although his clothes were made of excellent material, they were often old-fashioned and unattractive. Rumor had it that Truth sometimes walked naked in broad daylight through the village, to the shock and horror of all who saw him. Many villagers hated him, most people found his company quite uncomfortable, but some found him to be a man with a heart of gold, a steadfast, fearless friend.

It came to pass that the village where Truth and Lie lived fell upon hard times. For months beyond counting, not a drop of rain fell from heaven. The wells and the rivers dried up, the green grass and the leaves upon the trees withered and died. The land, once famed for the abundance of its yields of corn, millet, yams, potatoes, and cassava, stood desolate and bare. It could not sustain the people any more.

One day, Lie went to Truth and said, "I have run out of food and no one, not even my friends, will help me; and if I, the most popular man in the village, am hungry, you whom no one likes, must be starving. Let's bury our differences, whatever they are, and work together to save ourselves from death. Think of something for you and me to do, and let's do it."

Truth remained silent a moment, his chin cupped in the palm of his hand. Then he said, "What I am going to suggest will be distasteful to you, but I cannot think of anything else, given the desperate position we are in. Let's go begging. Perhaps those with a few provisions left will take pity on us."

Lie frowned at Truth's suggestion and remained deep in thought a moment, his lips bunched together, his arms folded tightly about his chest.

"That sounds wonderful, let's do it," he said, trying to sound cheerful and excited, whereas the look of distress on his face told a different story. Then with a faint, shamefaced smile, he added, "You won't mind taking the lead, will you?"

"No, not at all," Truth said. "After all, it is my idea."

With Truth leading the way and holding a begging bowl, the two companions of misfortune went begging.

"Give a little food, I pray, to Lie and me.
We've had nothing to eat, as you can see."

Truth intoned in a sorrowful voice as they went from house to house and from one village to another. A few people took pity and gave the two men a little food out of their own meager reserves, but most people drove them away empty-handed, saying simply, "How can we give you food when we ourselves are desperate for food?"

For days, Truth and Lie begged for food all over their village and in neighboring villages, but the food they collected each day was too little to feed even a baby.

"This isn't working," Truth said, shaking his head sadly and looking Lie in the eye.

"I wasn't going to say it," Lie said, "but now you've said it, something must be done about it."

"For days and days I've followed your lead. Now it is my turn to take the lead. Tomorrow at dawn, I shall knock on your door. You and I will go on a long journey. Follow me, do as I say, and together we shall work wonders!"

As soon as Lie went back home that night, he gathered hundreds of little gourds. Some he filled with dirt, some he filled with ashes, and some he filled with coal dust. The next day at dawn, he threw the gourds into a huge bag, slung it over his shoulder, and went knocking on Truth's door.

Before they set out on their journey, Lie started a whispered conversation with Truth, pointing to the huge bag he was carrying. Truth listened intently, a look of despair on his face. Whatever Lie was saying did not sound pleasant in his ears. Several times he turned away from Lie, but Lie was determined Truth should hear him out. As the whispered conversation went on, it looked as though the two companions were getting closer and closer to a compromise, for the look of despair on Truth's face vanished away, and was replaced by an expression of unease. Whatever his reservations, Truth seemed to have decided to give Lie the benefit of the doubt.

Soon, Truth and Lie left the village on a journey that Lie claimed would make them both rich and famous. They walked and walked until the sun stood high in the sky, its hot breath making the sand burn under their feet, and still they walked, taking breaks now and then, for Lie was often short of breath. They walked until the cool shades of evening spread over the earth, and still they walked. They went through many villages, but Lie wanted to keep going "To ensure the success of my plan," he told Truth, "I need to be in a village where no one knows me."

As darkness, dropping from the wings of night, slowly enveloped the whole land, they reached a village where no one had ever heard of them. "This is far enough," Lie said.

"Let's find out where the chief lives. Tomorrow the real adventure will begin...Remember," Lie warns, pressing a finger to his lips, "whatever happens, you shall not utter a word, unless you and I are alone together. Break that rule and we are finished!"

The next morning, a public crier was heard beating his drum and summoning the villagers to a gathering in the public arena. In no time at all, the arena was filled with men, women, and children jostling each other for a look at Lie and Truth sitting on either side of the village chief, a tall, slim man with a shaven head, clear brown eyes, and a beautiful smile. A hush fell on the multitude when the chief rose to his feet and, pointing at Truth and Lie, said, "These two men, Lie and Truth, have been my guests since last night. Lie is a medicine man with magical powers and Truth is his assistant. They have come to tell you what wonderful medicines they have made."

At those words, Lie got up, clutching the huge bag containing his gourds. He looked glorious in his bright-colored clothes. Truth got up too, but all eyes were fixed on Lie, because Truth, in his plain, dull-colored clothes, wasn't much to look at.

"As the chief has said," Lie intoned, "I am a medicine man with magical powers, and my assistant and I have brought a sample of the wonderful medicines we have prepared over many months of hard work. You may buy some if you want, but you don't have to."

So speaking, Lie made a great show of opening his big bag, brought out a gourd, and raised it high in the air. Everyone immediately looked upward, and while all eyes were glued to the gourd, Lie quickly shot Truth a stern, warning glance, and shouted, "This gourd contains medicine that will make all your wishes come true!" Exclamations of wonder greeted Lie's words, and he looked all around, enjoying the admiring gaze of the crowd. In quick succession, he brought out many more gourds, and explained their virtues. The crowd listened in open-mouthed wonderment.

"This one will make an old, old man strong and healthy like a young man not yet twenty. That one will make an ugly face smooth and radiant as a new moon. If you're searching for love, this one will bring you love. And if you want to get rich quick, that one will bring you easy money in plenty. If you have no children, this one will make you mothers and fathers of many. This one will make you invulnerable to arrows and bullets. And this one will protect you from death and disease, indefinitely." The crowd gasped in disbelief. As Lie extolled the virtues of his medicines, he stole a glance now and then at Truth. Truth was a terrible sight. He looked like a man suffering in silence and trying to keep his dignity as a swarm of bees stung him again and again.

When Lie finally fell silent, the crowd went wild, and it took the combined efforts of all the chief's guards to restrain them. In no time at, all of Lie's gourds of medicine had sold out, his huge bag was bulging with money, and people were clamoring for more. "We shall be back soon!" said Lie, smiling broadly, as he and Truth took leave of the villagers and their chief. "We shall be back soon!"

Lie and Truth went from village to village, and everywhere Lie sold as wonder-working medicine hundreds of gourds filled with dirt, ashes, and coal dust. Lie made a lot of money, and he and Truth lived very well. Truth had never eaten better all his life, but neither had he looked sicker. He grew fat, flabby, and sleepy-eyed.

As the days went by, he grew even fatter, flabbier, and more sleepy-eyed.

One day, as Truth stooped to take a drink from a pool of clear water, he stood thunderstruck at his own reflection. "What is wrong with me?" he wailed when he finally recovered his tongue. "What on earth is wrong with me? Once I was lean and strong and full of energy, but now I have grown fat and flabby and sleepy-eyed! I have turned into a grotesque image of myself!"

That night, as Lie was filling a fresh supply of gourds with dirt, ashes, and coal dust, Truth said:

> *You and I cannot dwell together—we must part.*
> *Life with you has made me sick to the heart.*
> *It has brought me wealth and good food,*
> *But it has really done me very little good.*
> *I must go now...to the places where we have been,*
> *And sold as magic remedy dirt, ashes, and coal dust.*
> *You're sure to hate me for it, but speak out I must.*
> *I cannot do otherwise. I simply have to come clean.*

Lie wanted to argue with Truth and tell him he was a fool, but there was in the voice of Truth a new note of conviction and self-assurance that robbed Lie of the power of speech. Nor could he look Truth in the eye, for after Truth spoke the last word, there came over Lie a superstitious fear that if he looked Truth in the eye, he would wither and die. So Lie held his peace and hung his head as Truth strode away. From that moment, Lie lived in mortal fear of an encounter with Truth. And although he traveled far and wide, and was exceedingly prosperous, he was careful never to come face to face with Truth.

Today, the children of Lie are to be found all over the globe. Some are called white lies, some big lies, some fat lies, and some flaming lies. They are generally good-looking like their father, and like him they suffer from heart disease and shortness of breath. Truth, too, has children beyond counting, and they live in every part of the world. Some are called plain truths, and some simple truths. Some are called harsh truths, and some unpleasant truths. Some are called bitter truths and some blazing truths. Except for a few named half-truths because of a certain resemblance to Lie, all of Truth's children bear a close likeness to Truth—lean, strong, fearless, and full of energy.

And just as Lie fears Truth, so, too, are the children of Lie terrified of the children of Truth. People say that there is nothing the children of Lie dread more than an encounter with the children of Truth, for the moment they see the children of Truth face to face, the children of Lie wither and die.

The Jar and the Necklace

Once upon a time there was a virtuous and God-fearing farmer. He was good and just and was known throughout the land as a man of great personal integrity; and because he was a man of God, he was blessed with good fortune and prosperity. His farm always yielded bumper harvests and never was he known to have had any trouble with pests or predatory animals.

As the years went by, there came upon him a longing for a wife. Before getting married, however, he decided to drop the name his parents had given him and adopt a new one. So it was the farmer let it be known that everyone should call him *Wa Min Yon Koa*, which means "Do Not Rejoice At Your Neighbor's Misfortune."

The name-change caused quite a stir in the farmer's community, for never before had a full-grown man renamed himself as he had done. What does the man mean by dropping the name he has borne all his life? What could have prompted such a strange decision? People were simply at a loss for an explanation, but the farmer had an explanation which laid all gossip to rest: he wanted to bear a name expressive of his character and his moral code.

Shortly after his adoption of a new name, the farmer got married. He loved his wife ardently and wholeheartedly and wanted to be loved in equal measure, but being a virtuous man who valued righteousness above all else, he craved more than his wife's love. So he told her:

"I love you beyond words, my beloved, and I cannot live without your love, but if you love me more than a woman ever loved a man, but have no place in your heart for kindness and compassion, your love will mean nothing at all. Clothe yourself in kindness and compassion and I shall account myself the happiest man on earth. What is more, we shall remain husband and wife for life."

The woman complied with her husband's wish and lived up to his expectations; and soon the couple won an enduring reputation for kindness and decency. Not long after their marriage, the farmer decided to rename his wife—and the new name, *Se Do We De*, which means "God's Will Be Done," stuck. As though by a common impulse, everyone in the community switched from the old name to the new.

The couple had everything going for them except that they had no children. Year after year, they prayed and hoped for a child, but neither son nor daughter was born to them. So the farmer took another wife and immediately gave her a new name.

Names and their meanings were a frequent topic for discussion between the farmer and his two wives, for he regarded names as significant statements about people. From time to time, he would call his wives to his room with a view to ensuring that their words and deeds were consistent with both his name and their own.

Addressing first his senior, then his junior wife, he would remind them of the meaning of their names and urge them to let those names be their guide day and night:

"*Se Do We De*—'God's Will Be Done.' Such is your name, and such it will remain. In your sleep and in your waking hours, bear in mind that God is supreme, that whether you are rich or poor, sick or in health, childless or the mother of children without number, God has a plan for you. However the fates may play, rough or smooth, bitter or sweet, whatever comes your way comes from God and must be accepted as the will of God."

"*Adinon Manzin*—'A Selfish Parent Is a Foolish Parent.' Such is your name and such it will remain. In your sleep and in your waking hours, whether on the pinnacle of triumph or in the pit of disaster, remember that a mother or a father must never try to be smarter than everyone else, nor seek to come out on top all the time. That a parent should not be afraid to be thought a fool sometimes, that parenthood requires humility, generosity of spirit, and goodwill towards everyone.

"Names are no laughing matter, nor are they supposed to be assigned at random. Names are meant to be a window into people's hearts, a key to their characters. The name defines the man. The name is the man. You lose your identity the moment you lose sight of your name. Play false to it and you turn into a stranger. Be true, therefore, to your names, for there is no greater disgrace than to play false to one's name."

The farmer could not wish for a more receptive audience, for the two women had complete trust in him and had pledged themselves to live by his principles.

One day, the farmer's second wife, *Adinon Manzin*, conceived. Her co-wife was happy for her, but she could not help thinking of her own barrenness. The good fortune of the one made the other yearn all the more for a child, and her yearning drove her to the very brink of loneliness and despair. But like a lifeline thrown to a drowning man, her husband's words would come back to her, and reminding herself of the meaning of her name, she would take comfort in the thought that God had made her childless for a purpose.

Not long after his younger wife got pregnant the farmer gave his elder wife a cola nut and, rather than eat or sell it, she buried it in the ground. The nut germinated and soon showed promise of growing into a healthy cola nut tree. *Se Do We De* could hardly contain her joy, for she saw the plant as a gift

God had sent to compensate for her barrenness; here at last was a gift of hope, the assurance that she was not going to live in vain. Long after her passing, the cola nut tree would stand as a monument to her memory, providing shade and nourishment to the members of the family from generation to generation.

The cola nut plant was soon threatened with mortal danger, however, and *Se Do We De*'s hopes turned to despair. As if driven by malice, the chickens and the goats of the neighborhood declared war on it, pecking and scratching and nibbling at it. *Adinon Manzin, Se Do We De*'s co-wife, was moved to pity and gave her a jar with a hole at the bottom. The jar was put over the plant for protection against the creatures trying to kill it.

Shortly afterwards, *Adinon Manzin* gave birth to an adorable baby girl, beautiful beyond compare. As a mark of her gratitude to her co-wife, *Se Do We De* gave the baby a gorgeous necklace which made her more beautiful still. As the girl grew, so did the cola nut plant. And soon it turned into a tall and graceful cola nut tree. In the season of the cola nut, its boughs were laden with big, delicious nuts that brought people flocking to its owner's doorstep. In the space of a few years, *Se Do We De* became one of the most prosperous cola nut merchants of the city.

Adinon Manzin saw her co-wife's increasing wealth and was overcome by jealousy. One day she went to *Se Do We De* and told her she wanted her jar back. The latter offered to give her a brand new jar and many other things besides, but her co-wife would settle for no more and no less than the very jar encircling the base of the cola nut tree. The farmer stepped in and tried to reason with his younger wife, but she was deaf to all reasoning. So the dispute was referred to the king and the two co-wives were summoned to his presence. Standing before the king, *Adinon Manzin* repeated her chilling request. Dropping to her knees, *Se Do We De* clasped her co-wife's feet, begging, pleading, and weeping for her to take another jar and spare her cola nut tree, but her pleading and her weeping were to no avail. So, on the orders of the king, the tree was cut down, and the jar restored to its owner.

Bereft of her cola nut tree, *Se Do We De* soon saw her wealth dwindle and vanish. In no time at all, she sank into poverty and unutterable despair. It was then the idea of her terrible retaliation was conceived. Rising one day at the first light of dawn, *Se Do We De* went to her co-wife and told her she wanted her necklace back.

"I have a necklace, more beautiful than your own, which I will give you as a substitute," *Adinon Manzin* replied.

"Nay," said the other, "I want no more and no less than the very necklace adorning your daughter's neck.

"But you cannot have your necklace," *Adinon Manzin* cried "You cannot have your necklace unless my daughter's head is cut off."

And *Se Do We De* replied, "I want my necklace back and I will suffer nothing to stand in the way."

The matter was referred to the king who, once again, summoned the two women to his court; and there, in the presence of the king and his attendants, *Se Do We De* repeated her terrible request. *Adinon Manzin* rolled in the dust, weeping, begging, and pleading for mercy, but *Se Do We De* had long turned from loving to hating, and from forgiving to bearing grudges. So, on the orders of the king, the beautiful lass was beheaded, amidst much wailing and gnashing of teeth, and the necklace adorning her neck returned to its owner, *Se Do We De*, "God's Will Be Done."

Louis Magbo

My story takes flight, over countries and kingdoms of long ago and alights on a farmer, Louis Magbo by name. In the village where he lived there was a forest that was considered the abode of spirits. From time immemorial, not a tree, not a blade of grass from that forest had ever been cut by human hands. People called it "The Sacred Forest." Everybody talked about it in hushed tones, and no one, except a man looking for trouble, would dare set foot in that forest without special protection.

But Louis Magbo was like no other man. He was a stubborn, reckless man to whom nothing was sacred.

"People say that the forest is the abode of spirits, but there are neither spirits nor ghosts except in the mind," he would boast. "Not a tree, not a blade of grass from that forest has ever been cut by human hands, but both the grass and the trees will have to make way for my farm!"

So, one day, shortly before the start of the rainy season, Louis Magbo took a machete and a hoe and went to the Sacred Forest. It was alive with birdsong, the chirping of crickets, and the cries of myriad creatures. The grass was green and matted, as it had been for ages. The trees, tall and imposing, stood close together like so many guards barring the way to a temple.

For a few moments Louis Magbo stood motionless, lost in wonder. Then, recovering himself, he quickly brought his machete out of his bag and, with grim determination, struck at a tree in front of him. All of a sudden, the birds, the crickets, and all the other creatures fell silent. And in the eerie stillness that had descended upon the forest, a voice asked, "Who is this man striking at my tree and what does he want?"

And Louis Magbo replied, "I am Louis Magbo, and I have come to clear the forest to make a farm."

And the voice said, "Friends, let's help this man clear the forest to make a farm."

At this, the stillness was shattered by the din of iron cutting into wood and of trees crashing to the ground.

In no time at all, the trees and the grass were cleared away and there lay before Louis Magbo a vast stretch of farmland where once there were big trees and lush grass.

Louis Magbo gazed at the land and was happy. But to the invisible, mysterious creatures who, in the twinkling of an eye, had cut the trees and cleared the grass, he gave not a thought.

A few days later, when rain signaled the start of the planting season, Louis Magbo and his wife took their hoes and a bagful of corn seeds and went to their farm; but no sooner had they brought their hoes down upon the land to till it than a voice asked:

"Who are these people cutting into my land with their hoes, and what do they want?"

And Louis Magbo replied, "I am Louis Magbo; my wife and I have come to till the soil to plant corn."

And the voice said, "Friends, let's help Louis Magbo and his wife till the soil and plant their corn."

All of a sudden, the air was filled with the harsh sound of iron biting into earth.

In no time at all, the land was covered with a thousand rows of furrows glistening with moisture and sown with corn.

Louis Magbo gazed at the land and was happy. But to the invisible, mysterious creatures who had tilled the soil and planted the corn, he gave not a thought.

Time passed, and out of the seeds that had been planted there grew tall, leafy stems. On these, there soon appeared, here and there, ears of corn topped by tufts of silky, yellowish hair. And when the wind blew, they swayed gently from side to side like mothers lulling their babies to sleep.

Louis Magbo's farm was beautiful to behold. No weeds ever grew on it, no monkeys ever touched the tall, leafy stems, and no worms ever gnawed at the silky-haired ears of corn. And Louis Magbo gazed at his farm and was happy. But to the invisible, mysterious creatures who were taking such good care of his farm, Louis Magbo gave not a thought.

Days went by, then weeks, and harvest time drew near. "It's time to check the ears of corn to see which are ripe and which are still unripe," Louis Magbo said, as he and his wife went to the farm one day.

But no sooner had Louis Magbo picked an ear of corn to check it for ripeness than a voice asked:

"Who is this man who is picking corn on my land, and what does he want?"

And Louis Magbo said, "I am Louis Magbo, and I have come to pick ears of corn to check them for ripeness."

And the voice said, "Friends, let's help Louis Magbo pick ears of corn to check them for ripeness.

All of a sudden, the air was filled with the sound of a thousand hands plucking ears of corn. In no time at all, all the leafy, corn-laden stems on Louis Magbo's farm were stripped bare and their ears of corn, the ripe and the unripe alike, lay in a towering mound in the middle of the farm .

Louis Magbo cast a sad, mournful look over his farm, and his heart filled with rage at the havoc the mysterious invisible creatures had wrought.

As he and his wife stood there, like people caught in a waking nightmare, a swarm of fleas, drawn by the smell of fresh-picked corn, set upon them, biting them mercilessly. Louis Magbo and his wife slapped themselves furiously on their legs, on their arms, on their backs—all over their bodies, as if to make the fleas pay for what the mysterious invisible creatures had done to their corn.

As they did, a voice asked, "Who are these people slapping themselves, and what do they want?"

And Louis Magbo said, "I am Louis Magbo, and my wife and I are slapping ourselves to kill the fleas that are biting us."

And the voice said, "Friends, let's slap Louis Magbo and his wife all over to kill the fleas that are biting them."

No sooner had the voice spoken than a thousand invisible hands slapped Louis Magbo and his wife again and again on the legs, on the arms, on the backs—all over their bodies—filling the air with a piercing, slapping sound.

Both husband and wife fell to the ground, writhing in agony and begging for mercy, but there was no mercy. The slapping went on and on and on until Louis Magbo and his wife lost consciousness and yielded up the ghost.

Denied the honor of a decent burial, they lay exposed for seven days to the hot glare of the sun, the chilling breath of night, to wind and rain, and everything that fed on carrion. With amazing speed their bones were picked clean and overgrown with weeds, but more amazing still was what happened on the seventh day. The farm and everything on it vanished from sight—the numberless rows of furrows, the towering mound of ears of corn, and the leafy stems that once bore them.

And in the twinkling of an eye, the Sacred Forest

reappeared. Once again, it was alive with birdsong, the chirping of crickets, and the cries of myriad creatures. Once again, the grass was green and matted, as it had been for ages. And once again, the trees, tall and imposing, stood close together, like so many guards barring the way to a temple.

The Prodigal Prince

My story takes flight, over countries and kingdoms of long ago and alights on a king. He was the most powerful king on earth, but he had no children. Neither his first wife, nor any of the numerous wives who followed, gave birth. Then one day, against all expectations, the king's eldest wife, who had long passed the childbearing age, conceived and brought forth a baby boy. The king was overjoyed, but for reasons no one could understand, he did not give the child a name. Two years later, his eldest wife fell pregnant again, to the astonishment of all, and gave birth to yet another boy. The king was overwhelmed with joy, but as with the first prince, he would not give the newborn a name.

The two princes grew and grew, and had everything a powerful and loving father could provide for his children. Soon they reached the age when they must leave their father's home and live on their own. The king gave each of them a bride and had two houses built: both were a day's journey from the royal city but only half a day's journey each from the other.

Then, the king called both princes and said:

"My children, the time has come when you must go forth from the palace and build a life for yourselves. Before I let you go, however, I want each of you to choose a name. Tomorrow at this hour come back and tell me your names."

The next day the elder prince told his father his name was going to be "My Father Will Provide." The king's head swelled with pride and his joy knew no bounds, for that name was a reminder, to friends and foes alike, of his awesome power and majesty. Then the king's second son told his father he wished to be called "God Will Provide." The king jumped up as if

40

stung by a scorpion. A shadow passed over his face, his hair stood on end, and he flew into a rage. How could his own son insult and humiliate him so! The name was an affront, an ugly stain upon his honor, and he was determined to chastise the ungrateful and irreverent prince.

So, the king drove "God Will Provide" and his bride out of the royal palace and confined them to the house he had assigned to them. Nothing did he give the unhappy, grief-stricken prince, not even a day's provisions.

"I shall give him nothing," he thundered. "Let him turn to God, whom he has put before me."

The king's treatment of "Father Will Provide" was very different, however. He loaded him with priceless gifts and had him and his bride accompanied to their new home with pomp and ceremony. For many years, "Father Will Provide" and his wife lived in the lap of luxury, and each day was a holiday in their mansion. "God Will Provide" and his wife, however, were dogged by hardship; they were hardworking and thrifty farmers, but they had great difficulty making both ends meet, especially in the long months preceding their first harvest.

One day "God Will Provide" decided to throw himself on his brother's mercy in order not to starve to death. So he journeyed to his brother's mansion and implored his assistance:

"Since you and I left our father's home," he said, " I have known nothing but hard luck. Now, in desperation, I have come to you for help. Please, have mercy on my wife and me, for without your help we will surely die of hunger."

"Why have you come to me for help?" his brother asked sarcastically, his eyes gleaming with malice and haughty pride.

"Doesn't God attend to your needs? Or has He turned His

back on you? Go to the pigsty over there, and help yourself to the food I have left for the pigs."

"God Will Provide" thanked him and betook himself to the pigsty, helped himself to the food provided for the pigs and returned home. He renewed his request whenever he and his wife were down to their last resources, for they had little luck with their farm, and "My Father Will Provide" invariably sent him to the pigsty.

One day, the king decided to give "My Father Will Provide" a gift that would make him one of the wealthiest men in the land. He took a papaya and, through a tiny cut, stuffed it full of "ayun," a precious stone much sought after in those days. Then, very skillfully, he sealed the fruit back to its original shape and appearance, and sent it to his favorite son along with other victuals and foodstuffs.

"My Father Will Provide" could hardly contain his irritation when he saw the papaya.

"What does my father mean by sending me a papaya! What has come over the old man! How can he forget I don't like papaya! Old age is surely a strange thing. Who knows what the old man is going to send me this time next year!" he cried and promptly ordered the fruit to be taken to the pigsty.

Shortly afterwards, "God Will Provide" arrived with a request for food. His brother sent him to the pigsty as usual and there he found the papaya and took it home. In the morning, "God Will Provide" asked his wife to cut the papaya up so they could take it to the farm and eat it for lunch. But when his wife struck the papaya with a machete, it sent off sparks.

"God Will Provide" laughed and laughed when his wife told him she could not cut the papaya. "Who has ever heard of a papaya sending off sparks," he asked. Bring the papaya and

I will show you that the sparks you saw were nothing but a figment of your imagination. But when "God Will Provide" split open the papaya, a myriad of "ayun", the most precious gem on earth, came spilling out!

Skipping and dancing for joy, the couple carefully collected the gems. That year their farm yielded a bumper crop, and within a few years, wealth and prosperity made "God Will Provide," his wife, and their children the envy of the people in their town and beyond. For all his prosperity and fame, however, "God Will Provide" remained a humble and unassuming man. Furthermore, he kept the habit of journeying to his brother's mansion once in a while to beg for food. Before going to his brother's house, he would take off his beautiful clothes and dress in rags.

Since "My Father Will Provide" had never been anywhere near where his brother was living, let alone pay him a visit, he had not the slightest idea what a wealthy farmer he had become.

So, whenever "God Will Provide" came to beg him for food, he would greet him with taunts and send him off to the pigsty. As soon as he was out of sight and out of earshot, "God Will Provide" would laugh and laugh until tears would come streaming down his cheeks.

One day, as he came to beg for food, his brother told him that their father had expressed a desire for his two sons to pay him a visit and tell him how they were doing.

"Woe is me!" "God Will Provide" cried out ironically. "The time has come when my shameful plight can no longer remain hidden from our father's eyes. Since he threw me out, I have been dogged by poverty and want. One after another, my dreams crumbled to dust, and all my laboring has been to no avail. I must now go to him and say, 'Father, I was a fool to have named myself "God Will Provide" and not a day has gone by without my heart filling with sorrow for the choice I have made. Please forgive me for being ungrateful and disrespectful and make me one of your slaves, for I no longer deserve to be treated as your son.'"

Then "God Will Provide" made his usual request for food and asked his brother to lend him one of his old costumes so he would be spared the humiliation of appearing before their father dressed in rags, and "My Father Will Provide" obliged.

On the appointed day, "My Father Will Provide" put a few bananas into a basket as a gift to his father and set out with his wife early in the morning. The king was delighted to see his son and daughter-in-law. But when "My Father Will Provide" presented him with the bananas he had brought, he took it as a joke, expecting more impressive tokens of his favorite son's love and gratitude to follow, but nothing followed. Then the king asked him if the bananas were all he had brought him as a gift, to which his son replied that the bananas were all he could afford.

It was then the roll of drums accompanied by voices singing in praise of the king was heard in the distance, to the king's relief and great joy. "I knew you had played a practical joke on me," the king exclaimed. "I knew you had a surprise in store for me and that the bananas you and my daughter-in-law had brought were the prelude to something far greater and more impressive, a gesture commensurate with my hopes and expectations. Your brother can bring bananas but not you, my own favorite son, whose prosperity and happiness must by now be plain for all to see."

"My Father Will Provide" was still groping for words when "God Will Provide" and his wife made their entry into the royal palace, splendidly attired, and followed by their children and a multitude of friends and servants bearing expensive gifts.

Like a man jolted out of a profound sleep and struggling to regain full control of his senses, the king looked around, stupefied. To the left he saw "My Father Will Provide," sitting with his hands between his knees and his head bowed, visibly shrinking from public view; his wife was next to him, trying to screen from the sight of the multitude a basketful of scrawny little bananas. To the right he saw "God Will Provide," his wife, and their children, all gorgeously appareled. Next to them were their numerous friends and well-wishers. Behind them were the servants "God Will Provide" had offered to put at the disposal of the king to help with various royal errands and chores. A little farther away were the gifts his son had brought: rolls of priceless fabrics, jewelry in gold and silver studded with diamonds, rubies, and emeralds, as well as carvings of breathtaking craftsmanship. In the courtyard the king caught a glimpse of the livestock his son had brought: cows, bulls, sheep, goats and rams, donkeys and horses.

It was then that he realized how differently "My Father Will Provide" and "God Will Provide" had fared, and how cruelly his calculations had been upset and his hopes and expectations disappointed. Rising to his feet, the king spoke:

"I am a fool! I am a fool! I am the greatest fool that ever sat on a throne and today my foolishness is plain for all to see! Other kings have children without number, but I have only two; and because one stroked my ego, I gave him love, affection, money, and all that money could buy. And because the other did not stroke my ego, I gave him nothing at all. I pampered and spoiled "My Father Will Provide" and spared no efforts in ensuring his well-being and prosperity, but I cast "God Will Provide" out on a cold and unfriendly world to face alone and unaided the slings and arrows of misfortune. From the evidence of my eyes, never have two princes confounded more thoroughly the designs and calculations of a king. The pariah prince has raised himself from the dust to the pinnacle of wealth and prosperity, and the prince charming has snatched hardship from the jaws of plenty. The wisdom, the courage, and the generosity of the one, the laziness, the improvidence, and the wickedness of the other show beyond a shadow of a doubt who of the two is the natural heir to the throne.

"This, then, is my appeal to 'God Will Provide' as he takes over the reins of power: Bear no grudges, nor seek to settle scores, but be merciful. Forgive me for hardening my heart against you and for casting you out like an orphan. Forgive all the insults and the humiliation you suffered at your brother's hands. Let there be reconciliation, peace, and goodwill between you, and may God and the spirits of the dead bless your reign. As for me, my reign is at an end. I hand over to you this day the royal crown. Rule wisely, and rule well."

Then, the king strode into the sacred chamber and, taking the lid off the calabash of doom, looked upon Death.

The Blind Man and the Lamp

Long ago, in a village whose name is now lost in the mists of time, there lived a blind man. One day he went to see his friend in a neighboring village and was overtaken by night.

As twilight fell and the shades of evening deepened into the gloom of night, the blind man said, "I must go now, for it is getting late."

"Why must you go now?" his friend asked in astonishment. "Is there no place in my house where you may lay your head?"

"You do not understand," the blind man replied. "I had not intended to stay the night here. Let me go."

The blind man's friend tried reasoning with him, but it was all in vain. The blind man's resolve was as steadfast as a rock, and there was nothing his friend could do about it.

As the blind man took leave of his friend, however, the latter gave him a lamp, saying, "Go well, my friend, and may the radiance of this lamp be a companion to you along the way."

The blind man frowned, thinking to himself, "What use can a lamp possibly be to me, who am blind? This is an insult." And while his lips mumbled words of thanks, his heart filled with the bitterness and rancor of wounded pride.

As soon as he and his friend parted company, the blind man smashed the lamp to the ground and went tapping, tapping his way into the heart of darkness.

The next day at dawn, the people in the blind man's village awoke to reports of the blind man having been knocked unconscious and severely injured following a head-on collision with a cyclist in the dead of night.

The blind man's friend couldn't believe his ears when the news reached him. "How on earth could that have happened? I gave him a lamp, did I not?" he wondered aloud, frowning in bewilderment.

Quickly, he set out for the home of the blind man whom he found laid up and groaning in pain.

"I gave you a lamp, did I not," he panted. "What went wrong?"

"I took your gesture as an insult, my friend, and in the bitterness of my heart, I smashed the lamp to the ground and went tapping, tapping my way into the heart of darkness," the blind man moaned.

"Oh, my friend," the friend cried, "pride goes before a fall. I gave you the lamp, not that you might see by it, but that others might see you by its light.

"Pride is the archenemy, and greater sorrows and misfortunes than this shall fall upon your head unless you curb your pride!"

"Say no more, my teacher, my friend," the blind man sobbed. "My pride has been humbled to the dust, but I am a greater man for it, though blind and crippled for life! Speak no more, my friend. In much wisdom is much grief."

The Most Delicious Food in the World

My story takes flight, over countries and kingdoms of long ago and alights on the king of Oyo. He was a very powerful king, and like many powerful people, he was greedy, selfish, and cunning. Never was he known to take on an enemy or attack a neighbor without defeating him. There was one neighbor, however, that he dared not pick a fight with, and that was the king of Chabe.

Now the kingdom of Chabe was rich beyond compare. It had boundless reserves of silver, gold, diamonds, and many other precious stones. Every year, its rich farmlands yielded abundant crops of corn, yams, cassava, potatoes, black-eyed peas, beans, tomatoes, and all kinds of vegetables. Its rivers and lakes had fish and crabs beyond measure, and in the unnumbered multitude of its orchards, all kinds of fruit trees abounded: mango trees, guava trees, avocado trees, orange trees, banana trees.

In spite of its vast wealth, Chabe had no army to speak of, however. And whenever the king of Oyo thought of the prosperity of the kingdom of Chabe, his eyes would glaze over with envy. If he should give the order, a handful of his warriors could take over that kingdom in the twinkling of an eye, but there was a slight difficulty in the path of his dream of conquest: From time beyond memory, the kingdom of Oyo and the kingdom of Chabe had been bound by ties of blood. Moreover, friendship between the kings of the two kingdoms had been passed down from one generation to another. In those days, violence against a relative, however distant, was frowned upon, but treachery against a friend was considered a very serious crime.

For a long time the king of Oyo searched and searched for an excuse to attack his neighbor and take possession of his vast wealth without drawing accusations of envy or treachery, but he could find none at all. One day, however, a bright idea occurred to him, and his face lit up with spiteful joy. He was going to ask his friend to solve a hard riddle. Riddle-solving contests were a popular pastime and an ancient tradition among the people of that region. When a man lost a riddle-solving contest, he might have to give up his house and even his wife. And a king who lost a contest would have to surrender part or all of his kingdom.

The riddle the king of Oyo was going to throw the king of Chabe was a riddle he knew he could never solve, "What is the most delicious food in the world?" If the king of Chabe said one thing, he would say another, and he would use the argument that would follow as an excuse to pick a fight with his friend and invade his kingdom. If, for example, the king of Chabe said in answer to the riddle that the most delicious food in the world was black-eyed peas seasoned with onion, salt and pepper, and served with palm oil and cassava flour, he would reply that rice served with smoked beef sauce was more delicious. If his friend should say that red corn paste served with grilled chicken seasoned with powdered shrimp, salt and pepper, and fresh tomatoes was the greatest food in the world, he would say that pounded yam served with greens and dried and salted bush-meat was greater. Whatever dish his friend put forward, he would counter with another. The resulting argument would give him an opportunity to wound his friend's pride and pick a fight with him.

The king of Oyo was so pleased with himself and so sure of the outcome of his wicked plot that he could hardly wait for dawn to break. And as he lay awake in bed, turning this way and that, he went over his plot down to the smallest detail, again and again, to make sure his friend was left with no means of escape.

The village roosters had hardly sounded the first chorus of kokoriokos in greeting to the new dawn when the king of Oyo summoned to his presence a dozen of his most trusted soldiers.

With fire in his eyes he told them, "Go to the king of Chabe immediately and tell him I request his answer to the following riddle: What is the most delicious food in the world? His answer to this riddle is of the greatest importance and he must let me have it before the setting of the sun."

The soldiers bowed to the king, touched their foreheads to the ground respectfully according to custom, and set out on their royal mission.

Moving at a brisk, relentless pace, the messengers reached the palace of the king of Chabe just as the sun was rising over the land, tipping the treetops with fire.

The king of Chabe listened carefully to their message and then, showing them to a spacious waiting room, he said:

"Your message has entered my ears and I will provide an answer to the king's riddle just as soon as I have attended to a certain royal business requiring immediate attention. Make yourselves at home. I will be with you shortly."

The king of Chabe was taken aback by his friend's message and the manner of its delivery. What does his friend mean by throwing him such a riddle and demanding his immediate response? How on earth is one to decide on the most delicious food in the world? Which food one chooses is a matter of taste, and in matters of taste one choice is as good as another. The more the king thought about it the more he was convinced of the impossibility of a definite solution to the riddle. Suspecting a scheme on the part of the king of Oyo to take over his kingdom, however, the king of Chabe decided to think very carefully before offering an answer.

As a matter of fact, his promise to the messengers to answer the riddle as soon as he had attended to the royal business at hand was no more than a ruse to buy time while he considered the answer to send the king of Oyo. And while the messengers waited, the king withdrew to an inner chamber of the palace to think.

They waited a long time, without food or water, and still the king was nowhere to be seen. The sun had barely lifted its face above the horizon when they arrived at the palace, and now it was standing high in the sky, smothering the whole land in its breath of fire, and still the king kept them waiting. From time to time a royal messenger would come to them with a message from the king begging them to bear with him a little while longer. It would have been a terrible breach of etiquette to express impatience with the king in any way. So they waited and waited while their stomachs burned and growled with hunger.

Then, just as they felt they couldn't bear the hunger a moment longer, half a dozen royal cooks burst into the room, carrying silver platters piled high with grilled corn on the cob. The corn was steaming hot and delicately seasoned with salt. Like a pack of hungry dogs chancing upon a cache of juicy bones, the starving warriors fell on the corn, eating ravenously, smacking their lips hungrily, as though the corn were the most delicious dish they had ever tasted. They ate until their stomachs stood out like boulders underneath their clothes, and still they went on eating. Then, just as they felt they were going to burst from excess of food, a long procession of royal cooks filed in and laid before the warriors a mouth-watering selection of dishes: pounded yam served with smoked fish sauce, red corn paste served with grilled chicken seasoned with pepper, fresh tomatoes, and powdered shrimp, black-eyed peas served with palm oil and cassava flour, steamed rice served with dried goatmeat sauce, and many other choice dishes.

The warriors surveyed the delicious dishes helplessly, wishing they could make room in their stomachs for more food. All they could do, however, was nibble at a dish here and a dish there. In the end they had to let the cooks take the food away, regretting that they had no spare stomachs to accommodate all the delicious dishes the king had lavished on them.

It was then that the king himself entered the room, apologized for the long delay in tending to them, and asked them to tell him again what the riddle was that their king wanted him to solve. And the warriors told him.

"Well," the king said in reply, smiling gently and stroking his beard thoughtfully:

"Within the last hour you have been served grilled corn on the cob, pounded yam and smoked fish sauce, red corn paste and grilled chicken seasoned with pepper, fresh tomatoes, and powdered shrimp, black-eyed peas with palm oil and cassava flour, steamed rice and dried goatmeat sauce, and many other dishes. Perhaps you could tell me which of these you have found the most delicious."

The warriors whispered briefly among themselves and then their spokesman answered, "Your royal highness has lavished on us a great many delicious dishes, but the trophy for the most delicious of all surely must go to the grilled corn."

"What is grilled corn compared with pounded yam and smoked fish sauce or steamed rice with dried goatmeat sauce?" the king exclaimed, affecting disbelief at the warriors' choice. "Surely you must agree that your choice is a most unlikely candidate for such an honor!"

"Grilled corn, your royal highness, may appear an unlikely choice compared to all the other fancy dishes," the spokesman replied, "but the hunger gnawing at our stomachs when the corn arrived made it the most delicious dish of all the dishes we have had the honor of tasting today."

"You have pointed the way to the answer to the riddle," the king crowed, beaming with joy. "Go back to your king and tell him that together you and I have solved the riddle: The food a man eats when he is at his hungriest is to him the best food of all. I say go and tell your king: Hunger has a seasoning power all its own, and can make a humble, commonplace food the most delicious dish on the face of the earth."

The sun was just sinking down to rest when the warriors returned home. With rising hope, the king of Oyo had watched the sun go down below the horizon. The king of Chabe had missed the deadline he, the king of Oyo, had set, and his fate had been sealed. Soon Chabe would be no more! The sun fading from view was the sun of Chabe's destiny, setting on Chabe's standing in the world as a prosperous, independent kingdom.

Such were the thoughts on the king's mind when the warriors came marching through the palace gates. With sinking heart, the king listened as they rendered a faithful account of the manner of their reception by the king of Chabe and his solution to the riddle. Long after the warriors had fallen silent, the king remained deep in thought, frowning in concentration. Try as hard as he might, however, he could find no fault with his friend's answer to his riddle.

"Yes," he cried at last, nodding to himself, "The king has

a point. Hunger indeed has a seasoning power all its own and can make of a humble, commonplace food the most delicious food on the face of the earth."

From that day onward, the king of Oyo renounced all attempts to take over the kingdom of Chabe. For many, many years, they lived in the closest friendship until, one after the other, they passed out of this world into the Great Beyond.

The Jar with a Thousand Holes
An Oral History of the People of Dahomey

Once upon a time, in the kingdom of Danxome, there lived a prince named Gakpe and his elder half-brother, Vidaho.

Gakpe was a cheery, kindhearted little boy with a smile as beautiful as the sparkle of sunshine on water, but Vidaho was hard and unsmiling, and his eyes were like burning coals.

One day, the king their father, old and ailing, called a people's meeting. And he stood, holding Gakpe up in his left arm while his right hand lay on Vidaho's shoulder, and he told his subjects:

> *My final hour is hurrying near, and when I am gone*
> *your hands shall be dipped in hot water.*
> *My people, be of good courage!*
> *As the wind blows and scatters last year's foliage*
> *So shall your ordeal, your rage, and your despair pass*
> *So shall your hands and your spirits be soothed at last*
> *And the rule of the brute shall give way to that of the sage!*

When the old king died, Vidaho was crowned king. It was the custom in those days for a new king to give himself a name, for the name defined the king, the name was the king.

And so it was that when the kingmaker asked the traditional question, "What is your name?" Vidaho replied, *"Adandozan Bo Fli Fli Glo*, which means: The angry man spreads his sleeping-mat and no man of woman born dare roll it up."

With his defiant name, the new king had drawn a line in the sand, and no one dared cross it. His eyes flamed red, his voice was like the roll of distant thunder, and the members of the royal council and all the people with them recoiled in fear. The king, like his name, was a terror to all.

His ministers, his counselors, and his friends could have no will and no desire except his own. If he said yes, they too must say yes; and if he said no, so must they. That was the law, and anyone who broke the law must lose his head.

Under his father's rule, indeed from the birth of the kingdom, the army was a friend of the people, its shield against foreign invasion. It was the greatest sadness of the late king's reign that he had failed to free his people from the domination of the Yoruba kingdom of Oyo. For a hundred years and more, the kingdom of Danxome had been paying tribute to its powerful neighbor to the east: every year, forty-one men, forty-one women, a thousand head of cattle, and countless rolls of precious fabric had to be handed over as a pledge of allegiance.

It was a common saying among the people that "the task the father had left undone would naturally fall to the son." The late king would have given up the very breath of life to put an end to Oyo's humiliation of Danxome, but sadly, he had to leave the task undone.

Under Adandozan's rule, the army turned into an enemy of the people. His soldiers would sooner put a barn to the torch or raze people's homes to the ground than face an army on the field of battle. The king thought nothing of the belief, widely held in his realm, that no king could wrestle with his own people and win.

To him, the power of a king was measured by the amount of pain he could inflict on his people. To make the air ring with blood-chilling peals of laughter from cronies as he made old men fight one another with their walking sticks, or to watch a strong man go mad with fear on being ordered to fight a raging bull with bare hands—nothing gave him greater joy than these.

The king, it seemed, had got drunk on power and resolved to make his subjects the sport and prey of his wicked desires. And a great fear settled on the kingdom, blighting the lives of children and grown-ups alike. Even the land seemed to have fallen under a curse, for rain would not fall, and farmers had little to show for their labors.

With great sadness Gakpe saw the terrible suffering his half-brother's rule had brought to the land. "I shall speak to my brother," said he, "though to speak is to stick my head into a beehive."

And Gakpe spoke to his half-brother, saying:

Does not the suffering in your realm touch you, my brother?
The cries sounding from one end of the land to the other?
As a crazed fly trapped in the middle of a pool of honey
Such is a king without restraint
Both the fly and the king shall be consumed by their folly!

Adandozan's eyes flashed with anger:

How dare you talk to me of flies caught in honey!
Of kings without restraint done in by their folly!
My rule is a mat spread over the face of the land!
No man of woman born can roll it up and stand!
Babbling fool, tomorrow your head shall roll
For speaking out of turn and without control!

And no sooner had the king spoken than Gakpe was bound hand and foot and thrown into a dark dungeon to await at dawn the executioner's keen-edged sword. But when at the appointed hour the king's guards came for the prisoner, all they found were bits of rope strewn all over the dungeon floor. Of the one they had come to get, there was no sign at all.

The king's wrath knew no bounds. "If you cannot find him, bring me his mother! I shall make one pay for the other!" he howled, his eyes blazing. In no time at all, Gakpe's mother, a tall, slender woman of majestic bearing, was led before the angry king and was told:

> *Your son has roused a bull to anger*
> *And now you must face the danger!*
> *For his cowardly, unmanly flight*
> *You'll have to pay a terrible price*

Seven days later, men, women, and children listened in stunned silence as the king's messengers walked the length and breadth of the kingdom, spreading the news of the king's terrible vengeance: Gakpe's mother had been sold into slavery!

The queen-mother sold into slavery! Who could believe it?

At various times in its history, their kingdom had mourned the loss of a prince, a great warrior, or a royal storyteller taken captive by the enemy and sold into slavery, but never in living memory had a king sold into slavery a member of his own family! In selling the queen-mother to a slave-merchant, their king had crossed a new threshold of wickedness, and people shuddered to think what deed of madness he would do next.

And they remembered the words the late king spoke to them just before he went from their midst:

> *Soon, your hands shall be dipped in hot water*
> *My people, be of good courage!*

But where could one find courage when the world stood on its head and every new dawn brought greater and more terrible anguish than the one before it? And as the people quietly mourned the queen-mother's plight, an eerie silence hung over the whole land. Not a birdsong was to be heard, the wind held its breath, the moon and the sun hid their faces behind a veil of clouds, and the stars lost their gleam of brightness.

One day, at the crack of dawn, a voice was heard in the capital, warning of a plot by Gakpe and a group of followers and summoning people to an emergency meeting at noon.

As dawn brightened into day, rumors of an impending battle between Gakpe and his half-brother filled the air, stirring the hearts of men, women, and children with hope. Didn't the late king foretell an end to their suffering?

As the wind blows and scatters last year's foliage
So shall your ordeal, your rage, and your despair pass
So shall your hands and your spirits be soothed at last
And the rule of the brute shall give way to that of the sage.

Surely the end was at hand.

At the appointed hour, the king's vast front yard was crowded with people jostling each other and exchanging in whispers the latest rumors about the king and the inevitable battle between him and Gakpe, the savior who would put an end to their suffering.

Soon, the king, his ministers, and his counselors came out and sat in the place of honor. The face of the king was lined with care, and he looked a little frightened, but the ministers and the members of the royal council looked composed, almost joyful, as though the fear on the king's face was to them a source of quiet delight.

Suddenly, Migan, the minister of justice, a tall, broad-shouldered man of few words, rose up and, quicker than a bolt of lightening hurled from the heavens, took off the king's shoes! There was a brief scuffle, but soon, the crowd, spellbound with amazement, saw the king standing with his head bowed in defeat, his hands tied behind his back! It was then that Migan was heard crying:

From this day onward, you shall be king no more!
A new rule do we crave. Yours is rotten to the core!

No sooner had Migan spoken than a prolonged crackle of rifle fire was heard in the distance, intermingled with voices singing the praises of Gakpe. Gakpe and his soldiers were on the march! The sound of gunfire and the prince's name had broken the spell that had held the crowd tongue-tied and rooted to the ground, and they went wild, chanting:

From this day onward, Adandozan shall be king no more!
Gapke is the king we crave! Adandozan is rotten to the core!

And as it chanted, the crowd rushed in the direction the voices praising Gakpe were coming from. There was a deafening roar followed by long drawn-out cheers, as Prince Gakpe came into view, carried shoulder-high, his face radiant with the promise of change.

"I have come bearing solace for the sorrowful and hope for the hopeless," Gapke told the assembled multitude. "A wounded healer, I have come to heal our fatherland and wipe it clean of the stain which has made it an object of reproach among the nations!"

While the prince spoke, the crowd fell silent and many wept quietly—for joy and for love—for they knew that the man holding out solace to the sorrowing multitude and healing to their wounded souls bore the greatest sorrow and the deepest wound of all—a mother sold into slavery!

As Gakpe fell silent, Migan came forward and laid the royal shoes at his feet. Then, kneeling down and touching his forehead to the ground three times, he asked the new king the traditional question—"What is your name?"

And the king replied, "I am Ghe the bird, whose flaming plumage never sets the bush on fire. Call me *Ghe di zo ma si gbe* or *Ghezo* for short."

Never was a royal name more soothing to a grieving people crying out for a loving, compassionate king! Like the light of a new dawn, the name of the new king had put to flight the dark shadow of the old king's name and spread hope where once there was fear, and joy where once there was sorrow.

The people sang and danced in celebration, and for a moment the cruel king and his rule of terror seemed like a bad dream dimly remembered in the light of day. And while they sang and danced, a few guards made ready to take the former king to a dungeon where he would await trial by a council of elders. But when they laid hands on him, he uttered a scream that cut the heart to the quick. In an instant the joyful noise and clamor of celebration was stilled, and the crowd froze in terror. Teeth bared and foaming at the mouth, the former king was fighting to fend off the guards! He could not hold out for long, however, for he was fighting with his hands tied behind his back. But when the soldiers finally overcame him and lifted him up to take him away, he uttered yet another terrible scream and dissolved into smoke!

As the people stood looking upward, their eyes glued to the black smoke drifting overhead, there was heard a blood-curdling bellow and an enormous bull came charging from behind the palace and made straight for the new king. Men, women, and children scattered like dead leaves blown by the wind, crying and screaming in terror. Ghezo rose to his feet, and warning everyone not to come between him and the beast, rushed forward and took the raging bull by the horns!

People held their breath as the mysterious bull and the new king fought, pushing, circling, and straining every muscle in a desperate fight to the finish. For a moment, the king's strength seemed to flag as he gasped for breath, and a shiver of fright went through the people. But then their king quickly went down on one knee, pressing down on the bull's neck with all his might, and twisting its horns. The bull uttered a thunderous bellow and went limp. A thousand cheers rose to the heavens as Ghezo wrestled the lifeless bull to the ground and raised his hands in triumph.

Amid popular rejoicing, Ghezo told his subjects the meaning of his fight with the bull. Just as he had wrestled the raging bull to the ground, he said, so would their enemies be laid low; so would their struggle to fulfil their destiny be crowned with glory. But the struggle would be long and hard, and it would stretch their strength, their courage, and their wisdom to the limit.

And he concluded, "A new dawn is breaking. The day we have all been praying for is at hand. Together, let's bind up the wounds of our fatherland. Together, let's mend its broken spirit and make it stand tall. Only then will this land live up to the hopes and expectations this new dawn brings."

That evening and all night long, rain came pouring down.

In the morning, for the first time in a long time, people awoke to a day of bright sunshine; and the earth, parched and stone-hard from long months of drought, lay glistening black with moisture. When night fell, the sky turned to a vast dome studded with a thousand shimmering pearls; and the moon, casting off its veil, set the earth aglow with its silvery radiance. The people were filled with wonder and their hearts sang with joy, for they knew then that the curse of the old order had passed and that the new king and the new order were a blessing upon the land.

But even as the people counted their blessings, the king considered the challenges facing his rule:

To free his mother from bondage and bring her back home! To make the kingdom of Danxome powerful enough to break the yoke of Yoruba domination his people had borne for years beyond counting!

"These are tasks that would strain the strength and stamina of a superman," he sighed, and a shadow of fear and self-doubt passed over his face. But then he remembered the words he spoke to his people the day they made him king, "Just as I have wrestled the raging bull to the ground, so will our enemies be laid low...so will our struggle...be crowned with glory." And from these words he drew new strength and energy.

Less than a year after Ghezo became king, he had fashioned the army into a powerful fighting force, which, for the first time, included women warriors. Those were the Amazons, whose very name lives on to this day as a symbol of bravery. And when the king led his army into battle against the Yorubas to secure the independence of his people, they scored a victory that has stood as one of the shining moments in the history of the land.

But even as people sang and danced in celebration, there came to him a vision of his mother in shackles, her face bathed in tears, crying to him:

My son Ghezo, Ghezo my son!
May God give you strength
to set me free from the sting of the lash
and the shackles of bondage,
that I may see the sights
and hear the sounds of home once again
before I go down to my grave!

"By God's will you will be free!" Ghezo muttered, his eyes flashing, his fists clenched tight. "You will be free though a thousand armies bar the way and the distance stretches to the ends of the earth!"

The next day at dawn, there came to the palace a slave merchant, De Souza by name, whom the king had befriended soon after his mother was sold into slavery. He was the king's special guest for a week, but the purpose of his visit was veiled in mystery.

But six months later, a joyful rumor spread through the land, touching the hearts of the king's subjects with a thrill of excitement: the queen-mother had been set free from captivity in a remote kingdom in the new world! De Souza, a speaker of many foreign tongues, had been sent on a special mission by the king to ensure her safe return home!

When the queen-mother actually came back a few weeks later, there were wild scenes of jubilation. So happy was the king that he and his mother danced *Atcha-Hun*, the traditional dance of celebration! That was the first time the king had danced in public!

"I have come out of slavery bearing special gifts," the queen-mother told the cheering crowd, "seeds for palm trees and coffee, precious exotic plants from Brazil, where I was sold into slavery!"

Then she thanked her son the king, De Souza his friend,

and all those who had worked to bring her back to the fatherland.

"Long live the king!" she concluded, "and may this land of ours enjoy peace and prosperity for evermore!"

The circumstances under which the queen-mother was set free were never fully revealed, but the popular imagination made up a story to match the heroic stature of the king. When the king's agents found out that the queen-mother was in Brazil, the story goes, the king sent the ruler of that land an ultimatum: "Let my mother go or face the might of my army!" The queen-mother was set free on the spot, and the king gave her countless bars of gold and seeds of precious exotic plants as compensation for her years of bondage!

Following the queen-mother's return, Danxome entered a long period of prosperity. Palm oil and coffee brought in much wealth. The kingdom expanded through various alliances and conquests. The king was loved and revered by all, the fame of the kingdom spread far and wide, and the people were happy.

Time passed, and the king drew near to the fringes of old age. But then, from the palace, there came reports of rivalry within the royal family and the royal inner circle for power and the king's favors. It wasn't long before telltale signs of ill-feeling among royal grandees started to show: relatives and advisors to the king ignoring each other in public, ministers, traditional chiefs, and military commanders staying away from official ceremonies to avoid being in each other's company.

The king was deeply worried, and all his subjects with him. "Unless my people stand together as one, they are doomed," the king thought to himself. "What can I do? Of all the challenges I have faced, this is the toughest! I have overpowered a raging bull and broken the yoke of foreign domination. Against the odds, I have brought my mother out of bondage and clothed this land in fame and glory; but my reign will count for nothing unless I make my people see the value of unity and harmony." And the king wrung his hands in despair as his pleas and those of the elders fell on deaf ears.

It was then the king had a wooden platform built in front of the palace and sent royal messengers throughout the kingdom to invite all his subjects to a special meeting. At the same time, a royal proclamation was issued commanding the attendance of all ministers, royal council members, members of the royal family, and military leaders, as well as traditional chiefs. On the appointed day, a crowd like no other in living memory gathered in front of the palace, making the air buzz with the murmur of a thousand voices.

A hush fell on the multitude when the king came out, holding aloft a beautifully crafted jar covered with a thousand holes. Striding onto the platform, the king called by name various members of his government, his military high command, the royal council, the royal family, and many traditional chiefs. Then he said, "He among you who can fill this jar with water without a drop leaking out, let him step onto the platform!"

He waited a few moments, fixing the people he had named with a confident, defiant look, but none came forward. Then, the king looked around at the multitude and repeated his challenge. Again, no one moved.

It was then that the king beckoned to the platform all the people he had named and many ordinary people besides and told them to stand together and stop with their fingers the holes in the jar. And when all the holes in the jar had been plugged, the king poured water into it and not a drop fell. Then he said, "Behold, our fatherland is like a jar covered with holes. Unless we stand together and put our fingers to its holes, it cannot hold the water of life."

King Ghezo lived and died long ago, but the words he spoke about the jar with a thousand holes live on in the memory of his people, guiding them along the pathways of nationhood. Benin, heir to the king's legacy, stands in history as the first African country to have made a peaceful transition from dictatorship to democracy. What other peoples have sought and sought in vain through revolution, war, and bloodshed, the people of Benin have achieved by drawing inspiration from the words King Ghezo spoke long ago about a jar with a thousand holes.

A Friend Is Gold

Long ago, in a remote village whose name is now lost in the mists of time, there lived twins, a brother and sister, Zinsou and Zinsa. They had neither father nor mother—they were still crawling on all fours when they lost them both. Their foster parents were mean and miserly and made them work like beasts of burden to earn their keep. Zinsou and Zinsa had to be on their feet at the first light of dawn, in fair weather or foul. There were piles of dishes to be cleaned, countless rooms to be swept, a dozen gigantic jars to be filled with water, mounds of dirt-blackened clothes to be washed, and numerous errands to run.

Nightfall always found them tired beyond endurance, but they were never allowed to lie down and sleep until witches started flying through the air amid the hooting of owls and the forlorn crying of birds of ill omen. Zinsou and Zinsa often did the chores and ran the errands with their stomachs growling and churning, for their foster parents gave them very little food. No relative ever took pity on them, and no children from the village ever befriended them.

They were not entirely without a friend, however. They had a big, smooth-haired dog, the most playful, friendly dog that ever lived. While their foster parents, their relatives, and the whole world seemed to have closed their hearts against them, the dog provided them with love and companionship. He often accompanied them on their errands, walking or running ahead of them, his tongue lolling out, and his ears perked up to guard against danger. No village bully ever dared lay a hand on them, and no evil-doer could come near them. And when the hunger gnawing at the twins' stomachs was more than they could bear, he would slip out into the bush and come back holding between his jaws a squirrel or a hare for them to eat. Because he was such a loving, devoted dog, Zinsou and Zinsa named him "Sika" which means "A Friend Is Gold."

One day, in the depth of a drought which had turned the village into a dust bowl and exhausted the villagers' last resources, Zinsou came upon a strange sight. On the edge of the village, outside a lone hut screened from public view by a fence of twigs, an old man sat all by himself. He looked well-fed and was whistling merrily. He seemed not to have a care in the world, and was quite unaware of Zinsou's approach.

"What on earth has kept this man so happy and carefree while the whole village is moaning and groaning from hunger? How has he managed to stay so plump and healthy when the strongest and the healthiest have long been reduced to mere skin and bones?" Zinsou wondered, treading carefully as he came closer. "But the man is blind!" he whispered to himself, his eyes widening with amazement, his mouth agape.

It was then that the man, catching hold of his stick, rose to his feet and waved it in the air, in the manner of a magician wielding a magic wand, and muttered a few inaudible words. Before Zinsou's very eyes, steaming, mouth-watering dishes materialized out of thin air and were laid by an invisible hand on a mat at the blind magician's feet: pounded yam swimming in a bowlful of fish stew, roast chicken, and red corn paste, rice and goatmeat sauce. The food's sweet aroma tickled Zinsou's nostrils, his mouth watered and his stomach growled.

Like a night-watchman suspecting the approach of a thief, the blind magician stiffened, his features hardening into a scowl. "Who is it?" he asked fiercely, clutching his stick and waving it wildly, his teeth clenched and his hair standing on end. Zinsou took a few steps backward, trembling all over, his heart racing out of control. "I say who is it!" the blind magician screamed again, stamping his feet and turning his head in all directions. "If I catch any intruder sharing my meal with me, I will make him pay dearly. A word to the wise is enough."

The blind magician's threats struck terror into Zinsou's heart, but the hunger burning his entrails was stronger than his fear, and he decided to try and outmaneuver the old man by stealth. Having listened in vain for the slightest sign of an intruder's presence, the blind magician sat down to dinner. But he kept muttering under his breath dire threats against "those villagers" who had treated him so cruelly and were forever scheming to take advantage of him. Quiet as a sprite, Zinsou inched his way forward, sat down opposite the angry magician, and proceeded to partake of his sumptuous dinner. For every mouthful he took, however, he put a handful of food into his bag. And when he finally ate his fill and stole away, Zinsa his sister and Sika their dog were treated to dishes tasty beyond compare.

Zinsa's joy knew no bounds, but her curiosity was even greater. Her imagination swarmed with a thousand questions as she tried to wheedle out of her brother the key to the puzzle of the unexpected food, but he seemed to have been sworn to secrecy. Every day, at a certain time in the evening, Zinsou would disappear mysteriously and come back shortly afterward, carrying in his bag delicious food to still his sister's and their dog's hunger. As time went by, Zinsa's curiosity grew red hot, and her importunities more desperate; but neither her cajoling nor her veiled threats made her brother yield his secret.

One night, while her brother was asleep, Zinsa made a

small hole in his bag and poured ashes into it. And when, the next day, evening came and Zinsou set out on his secret mission, Zinsa traced her brother's steps. Following the trail made by the ashes from Zinsou's bag, Zinsa came upon her brother sharing a meal with a blind man. Quickly stifling the exclamation of surprise that rose to her lips, she sat down quietly by her brother's side and proceeded to help herself to the food. She ate gluttonously, as though the dishes were about to take wing and fly away.

Suddenly, as she reached for a chunk of smoked fish, her fingers collided with the fingers of her unsuspecting host! Swift as a conjurer, the blind magician grabbed hold of his two uninvited guests, uttering a triumphant, blood-curdling shriek. "So I have caught you at last!" he crowed, his face steaming with rage, his teeth gleaming white in the gathering dusk. "I will make you pay a very heavy price. A lingering death shall you die, as a deterrent to further intrusions!"

In vain did Zinsou and Zinsa beg and plead. The blind magician was bent on retribution. As though drawing strength from his rage, he dragged them to the back of his hut and buried them up to the neck in a hole he had dug for that purpose. Sika, the twins' dog, who had witnessed the tragic turn of events, knew better than to draw the blind magician's attention to his presence, let alone challenge him.

But when the magician finally withdrew into his hut and went to sleep dreaming of his two captives howling with thirst and hunger and dying a lingering, excruciating death, Sika set to work. Scratching and pawing all night long, he removed the mass of sand and mud holding his two friends prisoner.

The news of the twins' rescue from the blind magician's hole of death spread like wildfire and sent men, women, and children flocking to the compound at the edge of the village.

The blind magician was nowhere to be found, but they saw the telltale hole and the towering mound of mud standing in mute testimony to the twins' lucky escape and their dog's heroic labor of love. The blind magician's house was ransacked, and search parties went scouring the surrounding forest. When he was finally ferreted out, they took him to the chief of the village along with the twins and Sika their dog.

"Why did you bury these children in a hole?" the chief asked the blind magician. "Surely you must have known that it is a crime to try to kill a human being. What have you to say in defense of what you did?"

"If it is a crime to try to kill a human being," the blind man replied, "what, I ask, is theft committed against a blind, defenseless man by members of a community which had cast him out in his hour of need? Seven years ago, when in quick succession my wife and my two children died, my crop failed, and I lost my eyesight to smallpox, not a soul gave me a helping hand. I would have been eaten by wild beasts or bitten by a deadly snake if a benevolent genie had not taken pity on me when I went into the forest seeking death. I acknowledge myself guilty of the charge laid against me, but what about those who turned their backs on a blind, helpless man?"

As the blind magician fell silent, a thousand exclamations of surprise and wonder went soaring through the air, for beneath the matted hair, the heavy beard, and the plumpness of the stranger, most recognized a long-lost, reclusive fellow villager. As though catching the magic of the moment, Sika broke away from the twins and, whimpering softly and wagging his tail, he licked the blind man all over. Zinsou and Zinsa joined their dog and held hands with the blind man. It was obvious to all present that a new family had been born, and the trial of the malicious outcast turned into a joyous celebration of reconciliation and friendship.

The twins and their newly adopted father were showered with praises and blessings, but the undisputed hero of the occasion was Sika, the wonder-dog who had rescued his friends from death and then forged a family link between them and the one who had intended to kill them. And so it was that the inhabitants of that village and people throughout the region came to embrace dogs, hitherto considered mere playthings for children, as steadfast friends. Nothing has proved them wrong ever since.

The Magic of Love

Long ago, back in those days when the oracle ruled the lives of our people, there lived a prince, the king's only son. Tall, slim, and well proportioned, he had sparkling white teeth, eyes dark and deep, and a complexion the color of honey. There was never a more handsome child born to a king. But his dazzling good looks were his father's despair, for the oracle had barred the prince from romantic love. "He shall never taste love of woman," the diviner said in a voice that brooked no argument, "for if he does, he will surely die." And the oracle's words were as thorns in his father's crown, for he knew not how to save his heir from death.

The king had a mansion built, and around the mansion seven concentric walls with a single, narrow gate in each. The first six gates were watched over day and night by fierce, colossal dogs, but the innermost gate was guarded by soldiers bristling with weapons. No woman was ever allowed access to the prince's mansion, and whenever the prince had to go out, he was accompanied by members of the royal guard and a young man named *Hotcheme*, which means "He Who Reads My Mind." *Hotcheme* was the prince's best friend and confidant who followed him everywhere, as a shadow follows a person.

All the women in the kingdom longed to be the prince's wife and would give up the very breath of life to have a word with him, but the prince's guards and *Hotcheme*, his inseparable companion, formed a barrier against which they beat their heads in vain. Among the women who were in love with the prince, there was one named Ahla, the loveliest and most beautiful of all. She had soft, abundant hair, a graceful

neck, smooth radiant skin, big bright eyes, long slender fingers, and shapely legs.

But Ahla was not merely a young woman of unsurpassed beauty; she was also gifted with a keen and resourceful mind and a strong will. One day, Ahla saw the prince at the marketplace and tried to approach him, but his guards and *Hotcheme* intercepted her and drove her away. Five times she tried to catch the prince's attention, and five times she was discovered and driven away. The sixth time, however, she got closer to the mark than ever before. Disguised as a man, Ahla broke through the security ring around the prince.

And while the guards were scrambling to stop her progress, she took off her disguise and unburdened herself of the special words she had carried in her heart all those years, "Handsome Prince, Ahla brings you greetings and craves a few words in return." Ahla's words sounded sweetly in the prince's ears and, turning round, he beheld the most beautiful woman in the whole world! He felt an impulse to hold her in his arms and whisper a few words in her ears, but remembering the words of the oracle, he restrained himself and turned to *Hotcheme* instead. True to his name, the latter read the prince's mind and said simply, "The prince accepts your greetings and would love to grant your wish, but he is not allowed to talk to women or have anything to do with them." Then the guards drove Ahla away.

That evening, she shadowed the prince until she found out where he lived. And in the still of night, while the whole city was sleeping, Ahla washed herself, put on beautiful clothes and glittering jewels and, wrapping a few pieces of corn paste in banana leaves, set out for the prince's seven-walled mansion. No woman on her wedding night felt greater trepidation, nor looked half as beautiful as she.

When she reached the entrance to the first of the seven walls enclosing the prince's abode, Ahla quickly threw some corn paste to the dogs to make them friendly, and passed through the opening. She did the same at the next five gates and soon reached the seventh gate. The gods themselves must have been smiling on Ahla that night, for the soldiers, whose fearsome reputation had kept intruders at bay, were all fast asleep.

As though walking on air, Ahla entered the prince's living room. Neither the prince nor *Hotcheme*, his constant companion, was anywhere to be seen. Guided by a faint, rustling sound, Ahla made for a room where she found the prince sitting in bed, as though robbed of sleep by a vision he knew not how to shake off. And while the prince gazed at Ahla in wonder and ecstasy, she broke into song:

Tell me, are you really a man? Is he really a man,
he who feels no tingling of the spine on seeing a woman?
What kind of a man is he who does not lose his mind
When he looks upon a woman, the finest of her kind?

The prince rose to his feet and advanced towards Ahla singing:

Are you really a woman, Ahla? Is she really a woman
she who loses control of herself the moment she sees a man?
What kind of a woman is she who is driven out of her mind
Upon seeing a man, though he be the handsomest of his kind?

Then, he enfolded Ahla in his arms, and for a few enchanted moments, they found themselves in a garden of delights more wonderful than anything either had ever known. But when Ahla finally came to herself, behold! the handsome prince was dead! Distraught and frightened, she covered him with a beautiful piece of cloth she had been wearing, and stealthily made her way out of the mansion.

At dawn, there sounded in the king's palace a roll of drums, mournful beyond endurance. In no time at all, amid much weeping and wailing, the heartbreaking tidings spread through the royal city and to the four corners of the kingdom: the heir to the throne, the king's only son, had been found dead in his bedroom at dawn. The king's diviner had consulted the oracle, and the royal family's suspicion was confirmed: a woman had gained access to the prince's bedroom in violation of the oracle's dictate and he was tempted to his death. The prince's guards and *Hotcheme*, his companion and confidant, were under arrest, but the temptress was nowhere to be found.

Towards evening, after all the mourners had gathered for the funeral, there came to the royal palace a stranger accompanied by forty-one hounds. Dressed in spotless white, he was unusually tall. He had bushy hair, beetling brows, and spoke with a deep, measured voice. "I am a hunter on my way home from the hunt," he said, "and I have come to beg a little food and water for myself and my companions."

After the stranger had eaten his fill and his forty-one hounds had been fed and watered, he asked his benefactors why they were in mourning, and they told him.

"Because you have been so kind to me and my hounds," he said "I will revive the prince, provided you pass the test to which I am going to submit you....Gather a lot of firewood, bring me barrels of palm oil, and wait for my instructions."

At the stranger's request, members of the royal guard made a towering pile of firewood with a wide opening in the middle. Then he laid the prince's body at the back of it and, dousing the firewood with palm oil, set it alight. And while flames and blazing sparks leaped high into the sky and the pile of firewood was turning to an incandescent furnace, the stranger spoke:

"Whoever shall walk through the blazing pile and hold the prince's hand will bring him back to life."

"I will bring him back to life, for he is my beloved son," the king said, pushing out his chest and beating it with his right hand. But he had barely strutted a few yards towards the fiery mound when, enveloped by a searing blast, he beat a hasty retreat, hiding his face partly from pain and partly from shame.

Then the mother came forward, tying a headcloth around her waist to signal her determination to succeed where the king, her husband, had failed. "I will go through that fire and save my beloved son," she said. "Didn't I carry him in my womb for nine whole months? If not I, who can save him?"

So speaking, she strode boldly towards the blazing pile of firewood. But like the king before her, she was unable to advance beyond a few yards; the heat from the fire was simply too much for her. Quickly retracing her steps, she went over to the king's side. The king took hold of her hand and, looking longingly into her eyes, said, "Be of good courage, my beloved, we will beget another son."

It was then that Ahla, who had joined the crowd of mourners and had witnessed the turn of events, came forward singing:

> *"I will die of shame if I fail to go through the fire*
> *and bring the prince back to life.*
> *His father, who boiled special roots for him when he was born,*
> *to keep him strong and healthy, could not save him.*
> *His mother, who carried him in her womb nine whole months*
> *and nursed him for years, she, too, ran away from the fire.*

May I never see the sun rise again if I, too,
run away from the fire!"

So singing, Ahla walked through the red-hot furnace and came back, holding hands with the handsome prince. A thousand exclamations of joy, wonder, and awe greeted the miraculous outcome of her ordeal. Amid expressions of gratitude to the hunter, the handsome prince's funeral ceremony turned into a joyful celebration of his union with Ahla who, through the magic of love, had tempted him to his death and brought him back to life again.

The Wise Old Man

Once upon a time, there lived a wise old man.
His hair was white as cotton,
his sight was dimmed with the passing of time,
and he walked with a stoop, leaning upon a stick.
So wise was he that men, women, and children
came from the four corners of the globe
to seek guidance and advice for relief from the stresses
and strains of daily living.
And never was anyone known to go to him and return
without a smile on his face and a song in his heart.

One day two naughty boys from a village nearby
decided to humiliate the old man.
"Agossou, let's go shame the old man," one boy said to the other.
"Let's catch a bird, and I will hide it in my hands behind my back
and we will go to the old man and I will say:
'Tell us, old man, whether this bird I am holding in my hands and hiding
behind my back is dead or alive.'
If he says the bird is alive, I will wring its neck and let it fall at his feet.
If he says the bird is dead, I will open my palms and let it fly into the sky."
The two boys found it a very good joke.
They smiled, and nodded, and winked at each other, caught a bird,
and set out for the old man's village.
When the old man saw them coming, he welcomed them with open arms.
Crying, "What good wind blows you here, my children, my friends!
Come and sit and take a sip of cool water from my well,
and then we shall eat and talk."
"No," said the boy who was holding the bird in his hands and hiding it
behind his back. We do not have time to take a sip of cool water from your well.

Nor can we sit and eat and talk.
You see, we have come bearing a question:
Could you ever tell us whether the bird is dead or alive,
that I am holding in my hands and hiding behind my back?"

The old man looked at the two boys a long time
and then looked far into the distance, as though he had seen there a vision
he could not put a name to.
Then he brought his sight to rest on the two boys
and held them in his gaze a long time.
Smiling gently, he said:
"My children, my friends, whether the bird is dead or alive that you are
holding in your hands, is in your hands, my friends."

This happened long ago, my friends, but what it teaches us is as old as the hills
and as new as the latest news story.
Whether you and I pursue our dreams to the uttermost bounds of our potential
for greatness, or whether we let all our gifts go to waste,
rests in our hands, my friends.
Whether we make our country great and a beacon unto the nations
or a laughing stock and a derision to the whole world is in our hands, my friends.
And whether we leave this world a little better than we found it,
or leave in our wake hatred, sorrow, and despair,
that, too, lies in our hands, my friends.

Notes

"Why Monkeys Live in Trees," a retelling of a tale from the Boko ethnic group in Northern Benin.

"Why the Sun Shines by Day and the Moon by Night," a retelling of a tale from the Fon ethnic group in southern and central Benin.

"Why Bee Makes Honey and Snake Crawls on Its Belly," a retelling of a tale from the Sahoue, an ethnic group in southwestern Benin.

"How Goat Got out of Trouble," a retelling of a tale from the Adja ethnic group in southwestern Benin.

"Truth and Lie," a retelling of a tale from the Mahi ethnic group in central Benin.

"The Jar and the Necklace," a retelling of a tale from the Fon ethnic group in central Benin.

"Louis Magbo," a retelling of a tale from the Mahi ethnic group in central Benin.

"The Prodigal Prince," a retelling of a tale from the Fon ethnic group in central Benin.

"The Blind Man and the Lamp," a retelling of a tale from the Aizo ethnic group in southern Benin.

"The Most Delicious Food in the World," a retelling of a tale from the Nagot ethnic group in central Benin.

"The Jar with a Thousand Holes," a retelling of a legend from the former kingdom of Dahomey.

"A Friend Is Gold," a retelling of a tale from the Fon ethnic group in central Benin.

"The Magic of Love," a retelling of a tale from the Mahi ethnic group in central Benin.

"The Wise Old Man," a retelling of a tale from the Nagot ethnic group in central Benin.

RAOUF MAMA is an internationally known multilingual storyteller who performs indigenous tales from his native Benin. His previous books include *Why Goats Smell Bad and Other Stories, Pearls of Wisdom*, and *The Barefoot Book of Tropical Tales*.

A graduate of the University of Michigan with an M.A. in English and a Ph.D. in English and Education, Dr. Mama teaches at Eastern Connecticut State University and is the recipient of numerous awards, including a Greater Hartford Arts Council Individual Artist Award and two artist fellowships from the Connecticut Commission on the Arts, which has also awarded him the title of Master Teaching Artist.

ANDY JONES is associate professor of art in painting and drawing. He was born in Raleigh, North Carolina, and received his MFA in painting and printmaking from Louisiana Tech University. Professor Jones has exhibited throughout the United States. He is the winner of the 1998 U.S. Mint Quarter Design Competition for Connecticut. His work can be found in many collections, including those at the United States Mint Archives, Connecticut State Capitol, Connecticut State University System, Eastern Connecticut State University, Oklahoma Memorial Archives, University of Maine, Presque Isle, Southwest Texas State University, and St. Andrews College, as well as private collections in the United States, England, and France.

CURBSTONE PRESS, INC.

is a nonprofit publishing house dedicated to literature that reflects a commitment to social change, with an emphasis on contemporary writing from Latino, Latin American and Vietnamese cultures. Curbstone presents writers who give voice to the unheard in a language that goes beyond denunciation to celebrate, honor and teach. Curbstone builds bridges between its writers and the public – from inner-city to rural areas, colleges to community centers, children to adults. Curbstone seeks out the highest aesthetic expression of the dedication to human rights and intercultural understanding: poetry, testimonies, novels, stories, and children's books.

This mission requires more than just producing books. It requires ensuring that as many people as possible learn about these books and read them. To achieve this, a large portion of Curbstone's schedule is dedicated to arranging tours and programs for its authors, working with public school and university teachers to enrich curricula, reaching out to underserved audiences by donating books and conducting readings and community programs, and promoting discussion in the media. It is only through these combined efforts that literature can truly make a difference.

Curbstone Press, like all nonprofit presses, depends on the support of individuals, foundations, and government agencies to bring you, the reader, works of literary merit and social significance which might not find a place in profit-driven publishing channels, and to bring the authors and their books into communities across the country. Our sincere thanks to the many individuals, foundations, and government agencies who have recently supported this endeavor: Community Foundation of Northeast Connecticut, Connecticut Commission on Culture & Tourism, Connecticut Humanities Council, Greater Hartford Arts Council, Hartford Courant Foundation, Lannan Foundation, National Endowment for the Arts, and the United Way of the Capital Area.

Please help to support Curbstone's efforts to present the diverse voices and views that make our culture richer. Tax-deductible donations can be made by check or credit card to:
Curbstone Press, 321 Jackson Street, Willimantic, CT 06226
phone: (860) 423-5110   fax: (860) 423-9242
www.curbstone.org